CAST OF CHARACTERS

FAMILY
SECRETS

*Five extraordinary siblings. One dangerous past.
Unlimited potential.*

Connor Quinn—Could the brilliant blind inventor be the extraordinary sibling thought dead all these years? He's devoted his life to helping abandoned children, but who will help him find out the truth about his own devastating past?

Alyssa Fielding—The former model-turned-educator knows something is keeping Connor from finding a family of his own, and she's certain she can show him the way....

Jake Ingram—He may have found another surprise sibling, but has he finally lost his fiancée forever?

Agnes Payne and Oliver Grimble—Could the sightless baby they'd cruelly cast aside bring about their own demise all these year later?

About the Author

MYRNA MACKENZIE

has a passion for learning new things, so she was immensely pleased when she was given the opportunity to write *Blind Attraction*, part of the FAMILY SECRETS series and a book that would lead her down new paths into some exciting research.

But research is only the beginning step of writing a novel, and she soon found herself lost in the struggle her characters faced. "As my hero and heroine, Connor and Alyssa, came alive on the page," Myrna says, "and I grew to realize how strong and complex and caring Connor was, I ached to see him refuse to allow anyone to touch his heart. And while independent, stubborn Alyssa was a match for him, would even her giving nature allow her to overcome the barriers that kept her and Connor apart? This was a story that was very emotionally satisfying for me. It was a joy to have the chance to witness Connor and Alyssa's journey toward a timeless love."

Myrna lives in the suburbs of Chicago with her husband and two teenaged sons, who have somehow managed to turn her into a cheering cross country/track and field superfan. Please visit her at her Web site at www.myrnamackenzie.com.

BLIND ATTRACTION

MYRNA MACKENZIE

Silhouette Books

Published by Silhouette Books

America's Publisher of Contemporary Romance

Special thanks and acknowledgment are given to Myrna Mackenzie for her contribution to the FAMILY SECRETS series.

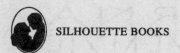

SILHOUETTE BOOKS

ISBN 0-373-61376-8

BLIND ATTRACTION

Visit Silhouette at www.eHarlequin.com

Printed in U.S.A.

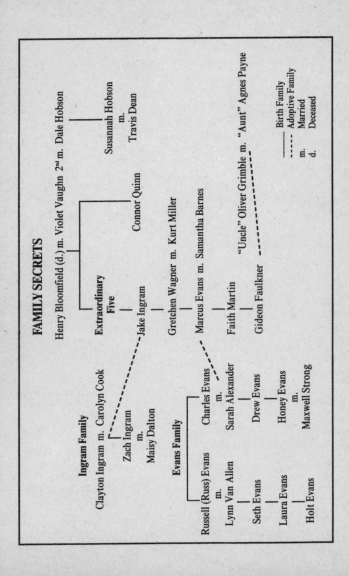

FAMILY SECRETS

Henry Bloomfield (d.) m. Violet Vaughn 2nd m. Dale Hobson

Susannah Hobson
m.
Travis Dean

Connor Quinn

Extraordinary Five

Jake Ingram

Gretchen Wagner m. Kurt Miller

Marcus Evans m. Samantha Barnes

Faith Martin

"Uncle" Oliver Grimble m. "Aunt" Agnes Payne

Gideon Faulkner

Ingram Family

Clayton Ingram m. Carolyn Cook

Zach Ingram
m.
Maisy Dalton

Evans Family

Charles Evans
m.
Sarah Alexander

Drew Evans

Honey Evans
m.
Maxwell Strong

Russell (Russ) Evans
m.
Lynn Van Allen

Seth Evans

Laura Evans

Holt Evans

———— Birth Family
-------- Adoptive Family
m.   Married
d.   Deceased

One

Connor Quinn kept himself seated in his leather office chair only by sheer force of will and by clamping his hands on the chair's arms. What he wanted to do was turn his back on this meeting, get up and walk out of the building and over the fields that surrounded Woodland Haven, the Boston orphanage he'd endowed and was now discussing. Or better yet, he'd like to head back to his company, Solutions Unlimited, and his inventions that required no human discourse. But what he really wanted to do was tear the top off his head, scream at the top of his lungs and beat his chest. And all because of a woman.

"Well, a woman and a temporarily misguided board of directors," he muttered beneath his breath, raking the fingers of one hand through his guide dog, Drifter's, silky fur.

Drifter's body shifted. He licked Connor's fingers and resumed his usual resting position on the floor next to his master's feet.

"She can't stay." Connor's voice was colder than it should have been, given the fact that his board of directors was a bit jumpy today, but then who the hell really cared when the welfare of kids was at stake. "Tell her you made a mistake."

The room filled with silence except for the soft whir of the central heating.

Finally a sigh sounded from across the room. Evelyn Wentworth. He recognized the way she let her breath out slowly, as if putting off the inevitable battle. "She has to stay."

Evelyn's tone was that of a woman who had lived a long life and been through many unpleasant situations. "Mr. Briggs left suddenly. Woodland Haven needs a new director now."

"I'm aware of that." Connor moved restlessly and felt Drifter's warm, quiet body beside him, the only calm being in the room. "But it won't be Alyssa Fielding."

"Connor," Gerald Banks began, clearing his throat, "in spite of her public persona, Ms. Fielding is highly qualified. We were lucky to get her, especially on such short notice and with you out of the country on business." A trace of resentment threaded through his words.

Connor blew out a breath. "Yes, I know my being unavailable was a problem. Doesn't matter. And we'll find someone else. Won't be your headache. *I'll* find someone."

The sound of a chair scraping and heavy footsteps circling the room signaled Barry Edwards's pacing. "Connor, we know you want the best for the orphanage, but... How shall I put this? You're asking too much. The last two directors have—"

"Left because I'm too demanding and a pain in the butt. Yes, I know that. I helped hire them. That didn't mean they were right for the job. They seemed right at first, but that was a mistake. Their careers mattered more to them than the kids. There were oversights. This time there are no mistakes, no oversights. Alyssa Fielding isn't coming to Woodland Haven.''

"Connor?" James Riley's voice bore traces of exasperation as well as something else. Amusement?

"What?"

"She's scheduled to arrive in two minutes."

Connor felt his wristwatch. Two minutes to ten. He'd barely been back two hours. "Hell, you could have waited."

"Not after the teachers threatened to strike if we didn't either bring you back to handle things or get someone in there."

Connor knew James was right. "Fair enough. I'll handle things now. You can all go. I'll let you know the outcome of the interview."

"There's a chance you'll keep her."

"No chance. If we let Alyssa Fielding in here, you know what will happen. Woodland Haven will be on the front pages of the tabloids. The paper will turn the orphanage into a freak show."

It was what he'd fought against ever since he'd taken over the facility. The last thing he wanted was for the Haven to become a hell for those kids. Having anyone notorious or famous associated with the orphanage was too big a risk.

That was part of the reason why he never let anyone know much about the inexplicable differences, other than his blindness, that separated him from the rest of the world. His colleagues may have suspected. They probably did, given the complex nature and the number of his inventions. He did have a bit of a reputation, in spite of his efforts to keep to himself. But no one really knew just how different he was. They weren't going to. Ever. He didn't want the publicity.

Not that publicity was his only reason for maintaining silence regarding his abilities, but all the other reasons were personal, and he wasn't about to go there again. Better to just concentrate on the current situation.

Woodland Haven was quiet; it was a refuge. It had to be that.

Which meant one thing was certain. Alyssa Fielding would enter and leave the Haven faster than the speed of sound.

"Mr. Quinn will see you now."

Alyssa thanked the receptionist and moved toward the office door the woman indicated just as a stream of people exited the same office. She recognized all of them, had interviewed with them just yesterday.

"Hello," she said.

Muffled greetings ensued, but not hearty greetings. As Evelyn Wentworth passed by, she took Alyssa's hand in both of hers.

"Don't let him cow you. He's in a heck of a bad mood."

A jolt of shock went through Alyssa. "I see." Which was, of course, a lie. She didn't see at all. Connor Quinn was the money behind Woodland Haven. She knew that much, and she knew that he had been out of town during both of her talks with the board. What she didn't know was why Evelyn was warning her about what should have been a routine get-acquainted meeting.

Well, no point in wasting time finding out. Alyssa squared her shoulders as Evelyn released her and exited the building.

She forced her once-famous legs to carry her into the room.

Connor Quinn rose when the door clicked shut behind her. "Ms. Fielding, I presume."

"Yes, Mr. Quinn. I'm pleased to meet you at last." Alyssa was glad to note that her voice came out clear and strong, but she wouldn't have been surprised if it hadn't. Connor Quinn was quite tall with raven-dark hair, his eyes hidden behind a pair of dark glasses. The dog at his feet was a beautiful golden retriever. Together they made a strikingly handsome pair, but neither of them was small, and Connor, at least, was imposing. A lot of man and dog to deal with. Not that she had any problem dealing with dogs or men, but she preferred her men affable, not hostile. And in spite of Connor Quinn's greeting, no smile lifted his lips. This wasn't going to be a "welcome to Woodland Haven" meeting.

Still, he held out his hand as she approached. A practiced move even if he hadn't calculated the time her faltering steps would take when she entered the room and held out his hand a bit too soon. Alyssa rushed forward and placed her hand in his grasp. For half a second skin slid against skin, her small hand in his much larger one. Something, almost a heat shock, a physical sensation of his flesh connecting with hers, hit her. She thought she saw a muscle tense in Connor Quinn's jaw, but she must have been mistaken, because they'd barely even made contact. He'd already released her and was motioning her to a chair.

"Have a seat, Ms. Fielding. We need to talk."

She sat, as did he. "We need to talk about when I'll begin my duties." No point in taking a defeatist attitude.

"About the fact that you won't be beginning your duties. I'm afraid there's been a mistake."

Alyssa tried to keep her breathing steady. She didn't want him to hear her voice shaking. "Then you don't need a new director for Woodland?"

"You know that we do. But I'm afraid my board was a bit hasty in choosing one."

"I was under the impression that the need was pressing." She pleated the material of her navy skirt between her thumb and forefinger, trying to remain calm. She'd worked very hard to make her place in her profession, and it hadn't been easy, given her past.

"The need is there," he admitted, "but it's still not a decision I can afford to make without reviewing all the possibilities."

His voice was low and firm...damning. Behind those concealing sunglasses that emphasized the rough angles of his face, he was like a dark, sexy wall of a man. And he was unreceptive. She knew that feeling and didn't like it.

"Would it be all right if you took off your glasses? I understand that someone can be legally blind and yet still see some things, and that glare can then be a problem with perception. Are they for glare?" she asked suddenly, shocked at her own audacity.

"I don't need them in the conventional sense." Which meant he needed them for some other reason. "Do they bother you?"

"Not really," she lied. She wanted to see his eyes.

He smiled slightly and without any real humor, but he removed the glasses. "Anything to make this easier for you," he said smoothly, and she hated the condescension in his voice.

His eyes were blue, a brilliant dark blue, the kind of blue a woman would never forget once she saw it. Unfocused but compelling. She'd thought seeing his eyes would make this interview easier, but now she saw her mistake. She twisted the band of her watch.

"Mr. Quinn," she said suddenly. "I have to tell you that you'd be making a mistake to let me get away." It was a bold statement, but then she had nothing to lose. "I come highly recommended from my last position in Chicago."

He ran one hand over his jaw. "I've read your résumé, Ms. Fielding. I know that you have all the requisite degrees and recommendations, but Woodland Haven isn't just any orphanage. Many of the children here have special needs. Most of them have known humiliation, rejection, ridicule. Anything that brings the possibility for that kind of thing closer to them is a danger. Are you denying that risk exists?"

Ah, now she understood. Alyssa closed her eyes and tightened her lips. "You're referring to my earlier career as a model."

"Not just any model, Ms. Fielding. A highly paid model, one who was sought after and whose face would be recognizable to most people."

"That was my former occupation, Mr. Quinn."

"So you've grown ugly in the intervening years, have you?"

"A loaded question, Mr. Quinn. If I say no, then I'm a vain woman who cares more about my appearance than the children at Woodland Haven. If I say yes, then I'm a..." She faltered.

"I believe the term would be you're a liar. For the record, I'm not calling you one. I'm not doubting that what you've put down on your résumé is true. I'm merely saying that our needs are different from most institutions."

"I'm not going to go around posing in front of the cameras, Mr. Quinn. That job served its purpose. It paid my way through college, but it's behind me. I'm older now."

"Not that old. You're only thirty."

He said it as if she were ten, as if modeling had stolen her brains. Or as if she had been allowed to go to college because she was pretty and had batted her eyelashes at the school administrators and slept her way to a degree.

Blind rage tore through Alyssa. She'd faced this kind of arrogance and bigotry before. Many times. When she'd been a young ugly duckling, her lack of looks had cost her. When she'd grown up and become pretty, her appearance had counted too much. She couldn't discount her appearance. It had paid the bills and paid them well, but she'd spent years being made to feel that if her beauty were taken from her, there would be nothing left but air, that she would revert to the lonely child she had been. Sometimes she wondered if she would ever really escape her past.

But that couldn't matter right now. What mattered was that she no longer cared about Connor Quinn's size or that he could probably call his dog on her if she dared to overstep her boundaries. Rising from her chair, she moved forward, leaning over the table just inches away from Connor. Her breathing was strained, harsh, loud in the silence.

Connor turned toward her and now she was hit with the full force of that magnetic visage. She refused to acknowledge how overpowered she felt.

"Mr. Quinn, I'd heard that you were an intelligent man, a mathematical genius, in fact. Your reputation seems to imply that, but a genius wouldn't be so biased. He'd look below the surface, he'd consider the facts and not jump to conclusions based on inferences. You have the right to let me go. Of course, you do, but you'd be making an enormous mistake."

For a second she thought she saw Connor's lips twitch, but she must have been wrong. She hoped she was wrong.

"You're not laughing at me, are you?" She placed her hands on her hips.

The movement in such close quarters must have caught his attention. "Are your hands actually on your hips, Ms. Fielding?"

"I'm upset, Mr. Quinn." But she straightened and took a deep breath.

"Obviously. Tell me, why do you want this job? Don't give me your conventional response."

That gave her pause. Her conventional response was the truth. She wanted to make a difference, and she thought she could do some good.

"I like my work," she said simply.

"You've worked with disadvantaged children before?"

"You know I haven't, but…a child is a child."

He frowned and opened his mouth.

"Wait," she said. "Let me finish. I know what you're going to say, that these children are different, that they have different needs, that they've lived lives that no ordinary child can imagine. That's true. Of course it's true, but at the heart of every child, any child, those with special needs or those who have been given every privilege and advantage in life, is simply the desire to be loved, to be accepted, to be valued. Are your children so different that they don't desire those things?"

He stood then. Alyssa was a tall woman, but he made her feel small. Standing this near to her, he made her feel dizzy and out of control. She had actually berated him, something she didn't ordinarily do, especially not where her employer was concerned. But damn it, she'd seen those kids, and they hadn't been valued enough by the previous directors. She knew that feeling, wanted to change that. She wanted this job, and she wanted to make those kids feel valued and accepted. Connor Quinn was keeping her from having what she wanted and from doing what she believed she could do. She could be an asset here. She could help.

"You think I'm an ass?" He leaned forward, his palms resting on the table as he stopped, his face only inches from hers as he dared her to make a mistake and say the words.

So she had lost already.

Alyssa felt the sick bite of defeat. She took a deep,

shuddery breath and closed her eyes, knowing she was surely headed down the wrong road and knowing that if she was going to do anything good for any child, she had to know how to be honest and she had to know how to fight.

"Yes, I do."

"Why?" He barked out the word. Well, at least she was still on her feet. He hadn't knocked her down, ordered her to leave, or sicced his dog on her.

"Because you claim to want what's best for your kids, but you're sending me away. I'll be what they need, Mr. Quinn. I'll fight for them. I'll even call you names if that's what it takes to get you to see that I won't back down where those children are concerned."

He stood there for a few minutes as if he was studying the situation. "That sounds good, but then you'd know that," he said. "A woman who ventures out into the world of modeling is used to supplying what is asked for, to performing for the camera. A model of your caliber is probably naturally a little bold, but more than boldness is needed here."

"I'll convince you."

"How?"

"Try me. Give me a trial period. You can even tell the kids I'm temporary."

"That will make your job much harder."

"If it's harder, then when I show you what I can do, you'll be that much more impressed."

"And what if you get bored? What if you leave? The kids have lost two directors in less than a year. They need stability, someone they can count on."

"I won't let you or anyone chase me away."

"I can't promise that I'll be an easy employer."

"I think we can both safely agree on that."

He shook his head. "The board is going to be highly amused if I let you stay for more than one day. And surprised."

"Oh, I don't know about that. They hired me because I promised them I'd be a tigress with the kids. You're bigger than the children I'll be working with, but the principle is still the same. Do what needs doing, never give up."

"That's what you believe?"

She started to nod, then realized that he couldn't see her. "Yes, I do."

"Ms. Fielding," he said, holding out his hand. "You're very naive. I'm probably going to regret doing this, but the truth is that I find myself without a director and with no chance of finding one overnight. So…all right, let's try it and see how it works. For a month. Just one month. If you're still interested."

"I am." She took his hand.

She was very interested…in showing Connor Quinn that while he might be a genius, he certainly didn't know all there was to know.

He was just the kind of arrogant male she'd learned to steer clear of, the kind who'd made her life hell many times, the kind—oh, yes—the kind that she disliked intensely.

And she had just spent the past few minutes convincing him to let her stay and work with him.

Maybe she *was* all beauty and air, after all, if she'd done something this foolish.

And maybe when all was said and done, Connor Quinn would be the one slinking away.

"So she charmed you, did she?" The smile in Evelyn Wentworth's voice was evident.

Connor wanted to answer her smile, but he couldn't. *Charmed* wasn't exactly the word he would have chosen. The truth was that Alyssa Fielding had affected him in ways he didn't want to examine. The husky tenor of her voice had seemed to stroke his skin. When their hands had touched, he'd maintained contact for as brief a period as possible, briefer even than he usually did, given his talents. But still, his body had nearly jolted as the always unbidden sensations of form and angles and curves and current had surged through him stronger than he'd grown used to. The surprise had almost made him lose control and catch her hand again to "see" the kinds of things that he knew unnerved people. And when she'd stood her ground and leaned over his desk, he'd admired her courage, but he'd also felt her warmth, breathed in her subtle jasmine scent, and he'd most definitely wanted to send her away posthaste.

"Thinking about it, Connor? *That* charming?"

He gave himself a mental shake. "I wouldn't jump to conclusions, Evelyn. Ms. Fielding's here on a trial basis only."

"But that wasn't what you intended earlier."

"She fought hard."

"Ah, and you admire that."

"It was a point in her favor, but I'm not convinced that I haven't made a mistake. She may be good, but the children at the Haven need more than good. They need outstanding, and they don't need someone who's used to glamour and prestige and who may be easily lured away when something more exciting comes along. Lots of people want to do something good. Very few have what it takes to see things through when things get unpleasant or boring.''

"So you only agreed to the trial period because she argued with you?'' Evelyn chuckled.

He took a deep breath. Evelyn never gave an inch. He still wasn't sure why he'd given in so easily. Something about Alyssa Fielding's voice, something beyond her fierce words. Definitely not her reputed beauty, her femininity or the silky sound of her voice. No, these were attributes he'd steered clear of for years. They wouldn't have won him over. He was impervious, used to denying his most male instincts to take and taste even when they rose high as they had when he'd felt Ms. Fielding's warm breath on his face.

"I said we'd try, Evelyn. I intend to be fair. One month, that's all. Any more than that and the children will get too attached to her.''

"Ah, and if she's only here a month, you won't have to have too much contact with her, will you?'' the elderly woman asked.

Exactly. "I'll do what's best for the kids, Evelyn. I promise you that much.''

"I never thought differently, Connor. You always do the right thing. I have faith in your expertise.''

So did he, if one was discussing the intricacies of physics or mathematics or computer technology. It was only in his dealings with people, especially women, where he'd taught himself to maintain a cool distance.

He might admire Alyssa Fielding's stubbornness, but if the sound of her voice, the heady, feminine scent of her and her risky act of standing up to him were considered, then she was a distraction he couldn't afford.

Still, he'd done what he came to the Haven to do. It was time to get back to his lab, to solitude, to the closed-off lifestyle that he preferred.

There was one thing Connor Quinn excelled at over all others: being alone. He liked things that way. Above all, he wanted and needed to be left alone.

Jake Ingram stared down at the lab report on his desk. In the margin, nearly illegible, were the scribblings of Henry Bloomfield, a genius, Jake's father, who had been killed many years ago.

"Genius begetting genius," Jake whispered, for Henry was also the father of Jake's four siblings he'd had no memory of until recently. Like him, they'd had their memories suppressed by their father's murderers and they'd all grown up separated from each other. Also like him, they were genetic superstars.

He'd only recently discovered their past and his, and only then because one of them, Gideon, had gone to the dark side and was now operating as Achilles. Achilles, like Jake and his siblings, had been genetically engineered to be capable of much more than any ordinary human. And Achilles was the mastermind of the recent World Bank Heist, a supreme act of theft and terror by a group known as the Coalition that had thrown the country into a panic and brought the genetic machinations of Jake's father to the forefront.

Now it was Jake's task to find Gideon, to restore

order to the international chaos that the WBH had wrought, but there was more to it than just business. Now that the WBH had brought the existence of his supersiblings, the Proteans, to his attention, Jake wanted his family desperately. He was proud and happy to have found all but Gideon so far.

Except...

"Five. There were only supposed to be five of us, dammit," he said, slamming his fist to the desk. What in hell was Henry thinking when he did this hideous thing?

"One more," Jake whispered. "There's still one more. The rejected one, born blind and therefore cast aside. The one that our stepmother believed to have died at birth."

That was the catch, Jake thought. The world thought his brother had died as an infant.

"I should just leave him alone." No one knew about this last sibling. There was no need to play with his life and bring him into this mess. And a dangerous mess it was, too.

His efforts to locate Gideon thus far had come up against walls and more walls. What was more, people's lives had been risked. There'd been kidnappings of innocents. Some of his siblings' lives had nearly been lost. His mother, Violet, had given her life. And Gideon, the mathematician, the technical wizard, the one at the heart of all this, the one who had ultimately been programmed and been born to take his blind brother's place...

"My missing brother, the unknown child, might be

the one to ferret Gideon out. He might be the one who holds the key.''

And he might not be able to do anything. His genetic programming had most likely not taken, just as Henry had believed. He probably would be of no use to justice's cause. Maybe he had other genetic defects that had gone unnoticed at his birth. He might not be capable of the simplest tasks, of anything at all. But if Jake dug him out from wherever he'd been all his life and the Coalition got wind of what he was trying to do, he might very well be signing his missing brother's death warrant. For now, as far as the world and the Coalition was concerned, his brother was unsung, unknown, safe.

Jake wanted him to stay safe.

Only these few scribbles in a single lab report mentioned him.

Jake swiped a hand through his hair. How could he be so sure this was the only record? He couldn't. He merely hoped the lab report bore the only mention of his missing triplet, because heaven help his brother if Oliver Grimble or Agnes Payne or their Coalition henchmen found him first.

Oliver and Agnes were the scientists who had coveted Henry's work and wanted to use it for their own criminal purposes. They had killed for it, had kidnapped Gideon and used his talents. Jake knew that they were capable of anything.

And in that moment, the decision was made.

''All right, it's done. No choice. I have to find him, and find him fast. Then I'll see if he has any of Gideon's abilities, or if Henry was right and the experiment with this sibling was a complete failure. If he has Gideon's

gift for numbers or technology, he might become another potential target and tool for the Coalition. Or he
might be an invaluable asset in my quest to end this
thing. Either way, I have to find him. Now. Before the
clock stops ticking and the Coalition realizes he's out
there. He was sent to an orphanage somewhere. The
only problem is…which one? Where in hell do I start
looking?''

Two

Connor lay in bed, feeling the morning's warmth grow, the welcome heat that filled the room and chased away the November chill. Scent drifted up from downstairs. Mrs. Welsh, his housekeeper, was cooking bacon and eggs again, even though he'd told her last night that he preferred something simple this morning. He almost smiled. Maybe she'd guessed that today he was going to need all his fortitude. More likely, she'd seen the slew of papers and empty coffee cups he'd left on his desk and realized he'd stayed up late to work, unable to chase down sleep.

Reluctantly he stretched bare arms over his head, then sat up, his feet braced on the wooden floor beside his bed. Hell, but he dreaded doing what he had to do. He'd had hangovers that left him feeling more prepared to deal with the day than yesterday's affair with Alyssa Fielding had.

No question, he didn't want to go near the woman again. What he wanted, Connor thought, was for someone to report to him that she wasn't doing her job properly, that she was all perfume and painted lips and pearly teeth and didn't fit with the kids. He wanted someone to let him know what was surely the truth, that like the others before her, she would soon reach the

conclusion that the task of dealing with truly needy
waifs was too demanding and not a boon to her trendy
career prospects. But that was the coward's way, and
besides, it wasn't fair to the children or to the other
employees. He'd agreed to the damned trial period despite his intense reservations, and now he owed it to the
kids to find out if his hunch had been right in the first
place. And right away.

No question, no excuses, he was going to have to be
the one to evaluate Alyssa Fielding and to initiate her
into Woodland Haven. And when the moment came, he
was going to have to be the one to ask her to leave.

Not that he hadn't done as much before. But before,
the kids weren't having one director after another fired
at them. What he ought to do, what he would do, was
start looking for someone who was the right sort, someone who would stay for a long time, long enough for
this crop of children to grow a bit and learn to trust a
little more. To learn that not everyone turned away.

He blanked out his own automatic response to that
last thought. Some of his kids might be damaged, but
none of them would be the way he had been. They
didn't have his dark nature, his propensity for brooding,
for measuring everything.

"They'll do better," he promised himself. "They'll
have more. And, yes, I'll start looking for the right director. Drifter, come."

Immediately his friend and helpmate was by his side.
Drifter was dependable, loyal, and Connor had no
doubts about his abilities.

"Maybe you should be the director of Woodland Haven, my friend," Connor said. "Then I wouldn't have

to worry about the kids at all. I could spend all my time on my inventions.''

And he wouldn't wake up in the middle of the night, wondering why the subtle scent of jasmine still lingered in his mind.

Alyssa slipped quietly into the room where she'd been told the children would be playing. She'd been up all night studying their files, but this would be her first chance to interact face-to-face. She wanted some time to study them unnoticed.

But as she entered the room, her eyes were immediately drawn to the far side of the room where a man lounged against the wall, his dog at his side.

The clicking of her heels on the floor halted abruptly as she came to a sudden, startled stop, and Connor Quinn angled his body in her direction.

''Ms. Fielding,'' he said, and she wondered how he could know for certain. ''I...wanted to be here to introduce you.''

His controlled stance dared her to call him on that statement, and she couldn't help smiling.

Daring more than she should, but less than she would if she allowed her anger to simmer to the surface, Alyssa stepped very close and lowered her voice.

''Odd, Mr. Quinn, I would have thought you wanted to be here to see if I made any mistakes, to perhaps discover if I'd brought along my camera crew to film me.''

To her surprise, his lips twisted up in a reluctant smile, and she was dismayed to note how devastating he was this way. "How do I know you didn't bring your crew?"

She wondered if the question was a test to see if he could fluster her. Most men had lost the ability to fluster her long ago. But Alyssa had a terrible suspicion that this man still could, no doubt because her heart was pounding rather harder than it should be. Still, she lifted her chin.

"You know there's no crew," she said firmly. "No whir of the cameras."

He nodded. "You think I have ulterior motives?"

"Don't you?"

His smile grew. Not a complete smile, but one that emphasized his masculinity, when that square jaw, that gorgeous dark hair and the muscles that tensed beneath his white shirt were already proof enough. "Drifter," he said, his voice low. "It seems she's on to us."

"A child would be on to you. You're not one to bother hiding your distrust, are you?"

He shrugged. "Subtlety isn't one of my virtues. Still, I know these children. I'll introduce you. Gather round, you young pirates," he called.

A soft giggle sounded behind Alyssa, and she turned to see a tiny blond girl in a miniature wheelchair. The girl expertly whirled in a circle and skidded to a stop beside Alyssa.

"That would be Letice," Connor said.

"I'm very pleased to meet you, Letice," Alyssa said, smiling down at the dimpled girl. "I like the hot-pink wheels."

"Mr. Quinn told me I could have my favorite color."

The other children began to crowd around, and Connor introduced them one by one: Kanika, who was blind; Wendy, a shy teenager; David, who squinted at her through his glasses. Alyssa made the rounds, murmuring hellos, touching when she was invited to touch, keeping a polite but friendly distance when she wasn't. She noticed that one very small boy, not much more than seven, hovered at Connor's knee but didn't come forward.

When she leaned over to say hello to him, he skittered back until he was completely behind Connor's body.

"And this is Joey," Connor said, just as if the little boy had come forward to make her acquaintance. "Joey can run like lightning. It's his gift."

"A fine gift," she agreed, lowering her voice coaxingly, but Joey remained where he was.

"Later," Connor mouthed as he turned slightly and smoothed the little boy's hair. He gave Joey the thumbs-up and smiled, and Joey took his hand for a second, then moved off to a corner of the room where a collection of toy trucks was waiting.

"Yes," she said softly. She'd read Joey's file. He'd been abandoned—more than once. No wonder he shied away from strangers.

But as she stood there watching him, suddenly a grubby hand was thrust her way, and Alyssa stared down into the eyes of a very dirty little boy, maybe eight or nine years old.

She reached forward to take the boy's hand, but Connor's much larger one came between them. "Bud, my lad, been romping in the dog pens this morning?"

Bud looked down at the dirt on his hands and clothes,

then looked up at Alyssa, his eyes wide with wonder. "Always be sure you take a bath, Ms. Fielding. Mr. Quinn will catch you every time. He can smell you ten miles away."

Alyssa looked up at Connor, who appeared to be on the verge of choking. "Bud, I'm sure that's... enlightening," he said. "Now, if you don't mind, go wash up quickly. Then come back and shake Ms. Fielding's hand."

"She probably don't mind a little dirt."

Now Alyssa was the one trying not to laugh. "I don't, but I think Mr. Quinn is most likely right. I have it on good authority that we're having a brownie break in a few minutes, and you'll want clean hands if you're going to eat."

There was a hesitation. She could tell that Bud was on the verge of saying that he didn't mind eating with dirty hands when Connor crossed his arms over that broad, imposing chest.

Bud sighed. "No point in arguing once he does that. Mr. Quinn means business."

She couldn't help herself. The man was so big, he was scary. The thought of a child being confronted by Connor Quinn was horrifying. "And what exactly does he do when he means business?"

"He doesn't let you near Drifter. Drifter's a working dog, you know, not to be played with. But when he's not working, sometimes Mr. Quinn lets some people talk to him and pet him a little. But not ones who don't listen when Mr. Quinn says to do something."

With that, Bud turned and ran out of the room, looking for water. The other children followed.

"That comment about how I enforce the rules. You thought maybe I brought out the whips and chains?"

Alyssa couldn't help taking a guilty deep breath. "I'm sorry. I can see that you have a rapport with the children, but— How shall I say this?"

"Just say it."

"You are a formidable-looking man, Mr. Quinn."

"It's the sightless eyes."

She blinked at his bluntness, barely holding back a gasp. His eyes were amazing, incredible. Surely some woman, most likely many more, had made a complete fool of herself over them.

"No. No, it's definitely the man. You're very…large and you do a good impression of a threatening thundercloud when you put your mind to it. I have the feeling you put your mind to it a lot."

He suddenly shifted on his feet, clearly uncomfortable with her scrutiny. "Enjoy your brownie break, Ms. Fielding."

He turned to go.

"Did I pass?"

He stilled. "It's only the first day," he said roughly.

"I would have thought, since you came here to see if I would get off to an acceptable start, that you'd want to stay a bit longer."

"I saw enough today. For now I want to check in on the new facilities we're building on the premises."

"I saw. It's a magnificent structure." Alyssa took a deep breath. "Would you mind if I tagged along?"

She would have sworn his body stiffened and he was going to leave without so much as an answer. "You have kids to care for and a brownie break coming up."

"Mrs. Jones and her aides informed me that they have the break in hand and that afterwards they've scheduled a lesson on insects and some games. I'll be back to mingle some more in just a short while. But this day is also for getting to know the Haven. When the children make the move to their new building, I'll want to be familiar with the grounds, all of them. I want to know everything I can know in order to be of benefit to my charges."

There, let him find some excuse to leave her behind now.

"It's a construction site. You're probably not dressed for it."

She sniffed. "You have not been a typical male thus far, Mr. Quinn, and that is such a typical male excuse."

"I only meant that it might be dangerous."

"You trust Drifter to guide you through?"

"Of course."

"Then I will, too. I'll follow in your footsteps."

"Wear sensible shoes."

"No problem. I hardly ever wear four-inch spikes with lacy straps anymore."

"Good. Though there are occasions where they're desirable, a construction site isn't one of them."

She didn't even want to think about when Connor Quinn might want a woman to wear skin-baring high heels.

"I don't think any woman who plans to get down-and-dirty with children would choose heels," she muttered as he turned to go and she fell into step behind him.

"You'd be surprised at how many professionals

know all the right terms and none of the nitty-gritty stuff," he said. "And how many people have preconceived notions about orphans that only serve to mess with the kids' heads and self-esteem."

"I don't intend to do any of that, Mr. Quinn."

"Good. What do you intend to do?"

"Care for them. Prepare them for whatever lies ahead."

"How will you know?"

"I won't. Neither will they. Does anyone? Did you?"

His steps slowed, stopped. "I'm not interested in my past. Only their future."

"I'll work to make sure they have a future. I'll protect them when necessary."

"As I admitted before, you know all the words," he said, his voice a soft caress, "but you should also know that I've heard the words before and misjudged. This time I need evidence, something more solid than lip service."

And what could she say to that rather humiliating statement when he was so…well, right? Only by showing him could she prove herself. Only by lasting out her month and demonstrating that his doubts were groundless could she make him believe.

"All right, I'll show you." The words came out loud, like a curse more than a promise, but it didn't seem to bother him.

"You do that." His voice was low and enticing, and he waited while she got her coat. They exited the building and walked across the grass toward the new facility in silence, Drifter slowing when they got near the construction site to wait for Connor to listen and instruct.

The outside of the building was nearly complete, all stark white and glass and polished oak, the roof sloping to an off-center angle with a long expanse of solar panels set like precious jewels in golden settings.

"Oh, it's beautiful," Alyssa said, taking a step forward. Immediately a loud siren began to blare in a repeating pattern of shrieks.

Alyssa jerked and jumped, bowling into Connor as Drifter dodged her feet. Strong arms caught her quickly, a dizzying bolt of something hot and breath-robbing shot through her as Connor's hands slid over her, and her back bumped against his chest.

Immediately he braced her, balanced her, let her go and stepped away.

"My apologies," he said, his voice strained. Did he mean for touching her and sending that heat zipping through her, or did he mean for the alarm? "Are you all right?"

She clenched her hands. "I'm…fine. It's all right, but I don't understand. How did I set off an alarm? There's nothing here, just a walkway."

He shrugged. "So it would seem, but that's misleading." Dropping to one knee, Connor ran his fingers along the edge of the walkway. "There are instruments set in here that shoot beams as you walk past, capturing…well, let's just say your essence on a spatial and, to some extent, on a cellular level. Anyone who has a legitimate reason to be here after hours will be in our database and won't set off the alarm. Anyone who doesn't belong will set off the alarm, triggering scanners in the roof that will not only take standard pictures, but will also calibrate details of weight, height and contours, which will then be relayed to computers in the building and, if triggered by an inside source, to the local police.''

"I'm impressed. I've never seen or even heard of such a system.''

He nodded. ''Sounds extreme, I know, but we have a duty to these kids, to make a safe place for them when all too often they haven't known enough safety in their lives. We need to keep unknown and possibly threatening elements out. In addition, although all of the kids are orphans, a few have made stops at relatives' homes along the way and some of them have been forcibly removed from their circumstances. They're here because they come from backgrounds where the adults in charge of protecting them have harmed them. We try to keep on hand as much info about those people as possible. This is just one way of making sure that no one slips in and harms an innocent.''

He was still at her feet. She looked down at him, and even though she was now the taller of the two, she still felt small and delicate next to him. When he rose, he was still near enough that she could feel his heat, and she sucked in a deep breath. Her mind began to whirl.

"I've heard that you invent things,'' she said. ''Is this alarm system yours?''

He shook his head as he led her toward the building. ''Wish I had invented it, but security is not my field. This is a new product from a company called Redcom Systems, which specializes in such things. I don't know as much about the company as I'd like, but I'm impressed. Although much of the technology used in this system is similar to that in other systems, the intricacy of the information-gathering devices located in the walkway is something out of the ordinary.''

"What *is* your field?" she asked as large, multifaceted glass doors slid open in front of them, revealing the interior of what would be the new Woodland Haven.

"This is." Connor held out his hand indicating the huge space before them. "The rest of the interior of the building is not nearly finished but there's enough here in the lobby and recreation area to give you an idea of what the completed product will be."

Product? What a cold name for what rose before her. Alyssa stepped forward into a spacious and sleek room that was all warm wood that curved and flowed. A wall of windows at one side let in the outside, revealing the fields and wooded area beyond. The floor was as yet uncarpeted, but built-in tables, bookcases and workspaces were already partly in place. A huge fireplace held a prominent place in the center of the room.

It was beautiful, but…

"A fireplace in a building with so many children?" she asked.

"The idea was to provide the kids with warmth and sensory appeal," he said. "A place where they could gather to read or hear stories or play board games. Something that said home. Stick your hand inside."

She frowned, unsure what she meant. "Inside?"

He seemed to hesitate, then he reached forward as if to touch her, but remembering the unnerving sensations that had coursed through her body both times they'd made physical contact, she took a deep breath. "Got it," and she reached forward to place her hand in the fireplace. When her fingertips were still a foot away, twin glass doors gently slid closed, blocking her entrance and protecting her from potential burns. The soft swoosh caught her by surprise.

"There's a backup generator in the event of a power outage. There's also a safety barrier inside the fireplace. If anything above a certain temperature falls or is moved outside that barrier, the doors automatically close, unless an adult overrides the controls."

"Ingenious."

His face was a mask. "Common sense." His voice gave away nothing.

"Show me more."

"If you like." Much of the room was still sawdust, emptiness and workers' tools, but Connor moved to a plush armchair, the only chair in the room, as if he'd memorized the location of every inch of the room. "Sit," he said, as if he was unused to asking for things. If he were a child, Alyssa thought, she'd insist he learn some manners. Unfortunately there was nothing of the child about Connor. He was a very grown-up male. His presence and his tone of voice demanded that she sit. He was her boss. It wouldn't hurt to humor him for now, she thought with a smile.

But she looked at the low, kid-height chair skeptically. "I'll try. I'm pretty tall."

"I've noticed."

Her lashes flew wide, and she looked up at him. He'd put his dark glasses back on as soon as they stepped outside, she supposed because there was a chance that they might run into people. She wondered whether the glasses were a shield for others or for himself.

"All right, here goes," she said, lowering herself into

the chair. Three seconds later the chair rose softly to a comfortable height.

She gave a small, startled shriek.

"Guess it worked." She could have sworn that was a hint of a smile trying to transform Connor's stern expression.

"How did it do that so perfectly?"

"It's computer driven. It sends out signals that assess your weight and your height and notes when your feet are solidly on the ground."

"Weight? I hope it doesn't share that information." She couldn't help laughing.

"It's a very discreet computer." For a moment she almost thought he was joining in with her joke, but his voice was so sober she couldn't tell. "There's a manual override, if you like. Press the button on the underside of either arm and tell it how much higher or lower you'd like to go in inches."

"Okay. Up three inches," she said softly, pressing the button, and the chair rose at her command. "Down four inches." Just as gently, it let her down.

"This is so great, but I don't understand why it needs my weight."

He leaned close and pressed the button. "Out five inches," he said, and the arms gently spread, giving her more room.

"How convenient. Do you sell these things to the public?" she asked.

"This is a prototype, although eventually the whole of the Haven will have them. The new building will be fitted with voice-controlled devices as well as braille markings on keypads to punch in commands for those who cannot use voice controls. All the fire alarms in the building will also be keyed to automatically signal the pagers of any hearing-impaired children, sending a warning vibration, alerting them to find the closest instructor or to leave the building.''

''So you're the brains behind this extraordinary building.''

She could have sworn she was paying him a compliment, but his expression had grown cooler than ever.

''I worked with the architect, but I'm not responsible for the building, just the devices.''

''Which are extraordinary.''

''Which are based on mathematical principles as well as technological necessity.''

His voice was carefully controlled, almost toneless, his lips stiff as he spoke. His statement implied that his inventions came out of a create-by-number kit, the kind of thing that any average citizen could envision and understand. She'd just bet that he'd repeated the same thing a hundred times or more. This building was so obviously unique. His inventions were clearly the work of a man of superior visions and skills.

So she was just going to pretend that he'd agreed with her and ignore his self-deprecating manner. Because when she looked at the lines of the building, she could see that everything fit, the building and the inventions inside. She was just betting that Connor had done more than simply work with the architect. And she could still remember the perfect, soft-glove fit of the chair. ''How do you know how to make everything fit so exactly? How do you fuse comfort and computer technology so precisely?''

"Practice." The word was uttered without expression, and so quickly that her words had barely exited her mouth before the answer had been given. It was as if he'd expected the question, as if he'd been asked it thousands of times before and didn't really want to answer.

Practice. She looked up at Connor Quinn and saw an extraordinarily handsome man who also had a lot going on behind those blue eyes. A man like that could be dangerous. A man who knew how to automatically program a chair to conform to a woman's body so that it felt like a welcome embrace had depths she didn't understand and probably shouldn't wander near.

"You should get back, Ms. Fielding," he said, and she didn't know if he was warning her as a man or as an employer.

"Yes. Thank you for the tour." And she reached out and touched his arm lightly. It was her way; she hadn't meant anything by it. But even though Connor's white shirt and black jacket separated her skin from his, she could feel him flinch, hear his breath hiss before he caught himself.

Immediately she stepped back. "I'm sorry. I didn't mean to touch without asking."

He turned to her with a frown and shook his head. "It was a natural gesture. Don't apologize."

But there was a thread of something in his voice that let her know she shouldn't touch again. There were obviously things she didn't know about Connor Quinn and never would know. No doubt it was best that way. If they were going to work together as benefactor and director of the Haven, a professional distance would be necessary, but…

"Would it be all right if you called me Alyssa? It's the kind of relationship I want the kids to have with me, and I'm not sure they'll feel comfortable doing that if you continue to call me Ms. Fielding. I won't expect this to be a reciprocal arrangement."

Connor called to Drifter and began to lead Alyssa back to the Haven. For a minute she didn't think he would answer her question.

"I'm a big believer in letting the director direct," he said, "as long as the intentions are good. So all right, we'll be Alyssa and Connor. My apologies for snapping at you earlier. Most people don't touch."

"I'm sorry. I shouldn't have—"

He waved an arm to shush her. "Most people are too afraid or nervous or uncomfortable."

He left it at that, and she didn't know what that meant. Was he simply trying to point out that most people weren't as forward as she was? He'd already indicated that her former profession, one that had required boldness, was not an asset. He'd already pointed out that she was different, not his idea of a director, but it was her boldness that had gotten her this job, and he had acknowledged as much.

The man was simply maddening. She wondered what he'd say if she touched him again. She would someday, but next time she'd warn him that it was coming.

See what he said to that.

Three

The headlines of the local paper were rife with the news of the falling stock market, a direct result of the World Bank Heist that had taken place last April and had wreaked havoc on the world's economy and sense of security. The president was still urging people to fight fear, but every day seemed to bring a new crisis, with normally sane people doing and saying crazy things, the result of a national edginess.

Alyssa flipped the page and saw a perfect example, the latest ramblings of a woman who claimed that she had been in her backyard one night and had seen one of the mutants, or Proteans, as they were called. The Proteans, Alyssa remembered from other news stories, were genetically engineered superchildren now grown to adulthood, who were rumored to be capable of everything from mind control to leaping tall buildings.

"All's right with the world. Everything's still as insane as ever," Alyssa muttered into her coffee cup as she thumbed the newspaper closed. It wasn't that she didn't care what happened to her country or that the world seemed to be on the verge of going up in flames, but right now her world had shrunk to the size of Woodland Haven. She had needy children to care for, and a hostile employer to worry about.

"Correction," she said. "I am not going to worry about Connor Quinn. I'm not even going to think about the man. He's immaterial."

Two hours later, Alyssa was on the verge of eating her words. Reluctantly.

"Mr. Quinn is such a sweetie," said Edwina Jones, the head teacher at the school, as she straightened a bow in Kanika's hair.

I had a pet hermit crab once that some might have considered sweet, Alyssa thought. Of course, Herman the crab had tried to pinch her fingers on a regular basis. Connor Quinn was not sweet. He was smart and judgmental and cold.

"He always makes sure that all the kids have extras like pretty hair ribbons and clothes that are considered cool, not just functional," Edwina continued just as if Alyssa had answered her.

Okay, the man might have a few good points where the kids were concerned, but he still had made unfair assumptions about her because she'd made her living as a model. People had been making assumptions about her all her life. She could never truly warm up to a person like that.

"How do I look, Alyssa?" Kanika asked.

Alyssa turned toward Kanika. In truth, the girl's little round face was somewhat homely. There were gaps between her teeth that would eventually need orthodontia, and she was at that ungainly age when her legs were starting to grow faster than the rest of her.

"You look lovely, Kanika," Alyssa said, and realized that she meant it. The little girl's radiant smile was beautiful, and in truth all children were beautiful. Just let anyone refute that within her hearing and she would tell them so.

But for now she had other plans. Today she was going to spend time getting to know the children a bit and letting them get used to having her around.

Nothing, especially not her chilly boss, was more important than that.

Alyssa gazed around the huge blue-and-cream room as Edwina gathered the teacher's aides and children together and assigned independent study projects for a science unit on simple machines. After a short lecture and question-and-answer session, the children split into groups. Some of them went off on their own and began to plan or even to jump right into their projects.

It always amazed her how very different each child could be, and this group was no exception, Alyssa thought, as she moved around the room, observing the children. She had read all their files and knew the basics of their backgrounds. Almost all of them had been born with a physical challenge or had originally been given into the care of adults who didn't value them. Their lives had not been ordinary or easy. Yet, many of them, most of them, leaped into the project with enthusiasm and abandon.

"Come look at this, Alyssa," Bud bellowed from across the room when he saw her watching him. "It's a supersonic people mover," he said of the bulky contraption he had quickly thrown together. Attached to wheels was a pile of blocks, at the top of which was a string with a magnet attached. As Alyssa watched, Bud swung his contraption around and picked up a fashion model doll that one of the girls had been carrying around earlier. The doll swung in the air, and the little girl squealed, ran over and grabbed her doll away.

"He stuck a nail in Jenny's head," the little girl said. "You're a jerk, Bud."

To Alyssa's surprise, Bud looked as if he'd been stung. "But…isn't it cool, Tina?"

"You made a hole in her head." Tina held the damaged doll out to him and gave a small sob. "You hurt my Jenny. You hurt her good."

A sudden and complete look of desperation crossed Bud's face. "I'll fix it. I will, Alyssa," he promised, looking as if he expected her to haul off and slug him any minute.

Alyssa plopped down on the floor next to the two children. "Come on," she said. "Let's see what can be done. Bud, next time ask for permission before you take anyone else's belongings. And, Tina, I think Jenny's going to be all right. She's got such thick, glossy hair that it covers the hole right up. We've all got little holes here and there, don't we? Look, I have two in my earlobes." And she removed her earrings to show the little girl.

Tina nodded, but Alyssa could tell that she wasn't convinced. Bud looked stricken. "I'm sorry, Tina. I just didn't think. I never think," he said, and his voice was angry. It was the voice of an adult. Alyssa was sure it was a voice he'd heard before from other adults. "Here, I'll give you one of my cars and you can bash a big old hole in it. You choose the one you want."

For a minute Alyssa thought that Tina was going to rush over with Bud and do as he suggested, but then the little girl turned to look at Alyssa's ears. "Maybe

you could make two more holes," she told Bud.
"Where her ears are. I could make her some earrings.
But make the holes little and don't pick her up with a
magnet anymore."

"I won't," Bud promised. He started to pick up
Tina's doll to make the holes. Alyssa caught the children's attention.

"Maybe that would be a good spare-time project,"
she said. "Something fun to do later. For now you've
both got work to do, I think."

"Yes, Alyssa," they both said, but their eyes were
eager. Probably with visions of piercing the poor doll's
ears, Alyssa thought with some amusement, remembering the awful things she'd done to her own dolls when
she was small.

"By the way, Bud," she said, pointing to his people
mover. "It *was* a clever idea. I'll bet you can come up
with something else just as clever."

He raised a superior eyebrow. "No problem. That
was nothing. Just practice."

For a minute, he sounded like Connor. Alyssa wondered just how much time Connor spent with these children. Probably not that much. He did have his own business to run, after all. This was probably just a charity
for him. She'd met many powerful men who were fig-
ureheads of boards, who used their money for good to
get tax write-offs and to improve their images. She refused to think of the building next door. Like Bud, it
was probably just a toy for Connor, a place to test his
ideas.

A short time later, though, Alyssa almost wished
Connor were here. All of the children had settled into

their projects, but when she turned and saw Joey, he was seated next to Edwina, staring off into space as the kindhearted woman tried to interest him in a variety of mediums she'd laid out in front of him. There was clay, paints and paper, red and yellow building blocks, blue and green building sticks and wheels of every size and color. Joey didn't even seem to notice.

Alyssa started to cross the room. She saw Davey, a shy boy of fourteen with thick glasses and kind eyes, watching and she smiled at him. He blushed and smiled and turned back to his papier-mâché rocket.

Alyssa continued on across to Joey and Edwina. She looked questioningly at Edwina, who rose and shook her head. She motioned Alyssa out into the hallway. "He's been like this for days," she said. "Another couple took him home. They brought him back the very same night. Joey sometimes throws tantrums," she said. "Every time a couple has come to adopt him."

"Counseling?"

"Every day. He won't talk about it to anyone. No one can reach him."

Alyssa nodded, remembering what she'd read in Joey's file. His parents had abandoned him and left him at Woodland Haven two years ago. They'd claimed they couldn't afford to keep him, though they had held on to their other children.

A vision of Joey cowering behind Connor nagged at her.

"He talks to Connor?" she asked. Joey hadn't actually spoken to Connor that day, but he had clearly trusted him.

"Amazingly, yes."

"I wonder why."

But the friendly face of Edwina suddenly went cool and blank. "Who knows why bonds are formed between two people?"

Alyssa didn't know what Edwina knew that she didn't know, but she was determined to find out, and she was determined to reach Joey.

Quietly she went over and knelt by him. "Sometimes we just have to let things sit for a while before we're ready to do them," she said. "I'll bet you have lots of good ideas in your head. When you get ready to share, I'd like to see them."

For a second she thought she saw him blink. Then he pulled deeper into his shell. She could almost feel his shoulders drawing tight as he leaned away from her.

And why not? she thought. He'd been abandoned, he'd been declared deficient and been sent back by several sets of parents. He'd seen two directors before her come and go. He and Connor had no reason to believe that she would break the pattern.

She knew from experience never to offer promises when only actions would do.

"When you're ready, Joey," she repeated softly, rising. "I'll be patient." But would she? She had never been a patient person. When she'd been an ugly duckling teen, unwanted in the orphanage, she'd wanted to prove that she didn't care. And when she'd grown pretty and become a model and realized that people were still judging her only by her appearance, she'd sworn she would prove that she was more. For many years she had been proud, defiant and angry. Ever since her parents died, when she was thirteen, and she'd realized that the only people who loved and valued her had passed on, she'd spent far too much of her life vowing to prove one thing or another to various people.

Now she wanted to prove something to Connor. And she wanted to do it now.

But she couldn't. She wasn't the important person here. Joey was. Bud was. Tina and Letice and Kanika and Davey and all the others. They were who mattered, their lives, their futures.

And her feelings about her boss couldn't be important.

Alyssa's dreams were restless ones, the ones where she was alone, always alone with no hope of ever being anything else. The ones she'd been dreaming since she was a teenager. She turned in her sleep and had just turned again when she heard a loud cry and then muffled voices. Another wrenching cry. Shuffling.

Alyssa sat bolt upright, her heart racing as she clenched the sheets. She shoved her tangled hair back over her shoulders, stumbled from bed and threw on a robe. Running down the hall and down the stairs barefoot, she slid into the playroom.

Joey was waving his arms, his little face red as he screamed. "Don't come near me. Don't come near me." He rushed toward the window as if he would climb over the sill and go running off into the night.

Alyssa's face blanched as she thought of the forest that lay beyond the fields outside the Haven. During the day the trees were lovely. At night she could only think they would be frightening for a child and make it all but impossible for a search-and-rescue team.

"Now, love, hush. Shh, I'm here. You're safe, you're cared for," Mrs. Morrissey cooed. The plump motherly woman was the Haven's housekeeper and nighttime housemother, and Alyssa had been told that all the children loved her. She'd come here after her own five children were grown and her husband had died. Her voice was calm, but worry swam in her eyes.

Tension nested in every muscle of Joey's wiry body as he danced from one foot to another.

"Joey, it's all right. You can stay here tonight in the playroom, if you like," Alyssa said softly. "You don't have to sleep in your bed. I'll bring quilts for the couch. You can stay here with the toys."

"Yes, love, that'll do," Mrs. Morrissey agreed. "Will that make you happy?"

Alyssa took the tiniest step toward Joey. His scream was pitiful, high-pitched and weak. He was shaking, clearly scared. Alone in his misery. No child that young should be this frightened or feel this sense of isolation. Something had to be done. What?

Without thought, Alyssa spoke. "Would you like me to see if Connor will come? Mr. Quinn," she corrected herself, remembering that Bud had called Connor that.

Like a laser beam, Joey's eyes pierced hers. He didn't say yes, but he didn't say no, either. And he didn't scream.

"Joey?"

A nod, barely there, very sharp, was her only answer. She turned to Mrs. Morrissey, her eyes questioning.

"Oh dear, I've never called him at night. I've never called him at all. He just comes. Now and then."

A deep sense of dread filled Alyssa's soul. What had

she promised? What if tonight wasn't a "now and then" and Connor refused? Or what if he was busy, had company, or even a woman in his bed? Most likely, the fact that she'd called him in at the first sign of a problem wasn't going to win any points with the man.

But she looked at the small bit of hope battling with dread in Joey's eyes and she made up her mind.

"I'll call. Mrs. Morrissey will stay with you, Joey," she said.

The little boy didn't answer. He sat down cross-legged and faced the corner of the room.

"Please come," Alyssa whispered, and she realized that she was sending a silent prayer to Connor.

The shrill ringing of his bedside phone broke the stillness of the night. No one ever called him at home except for his business manager, and it had been a long time since the phone had rung after office hours.

"This better be good," he rasped into the receiver, pushing himself over onto his elbow. The sheet fell away from his naked torso. He scrubbed one hand back through his hair.

For a second there was a hesitation, and he thought there might be a prank caller on the other end of the line.

"Hello," he growled.

"Connor? It's Alyssa. We need you. It's Joey."

Immediately Connor was alert. "Is he hurt?"

"Inside. He's scared. He's screaming. He won't let anyone near him and he's showing signs of wanting to run."

"I'll be right over," he said, but the last word was

faint. A thud sounded, and all she could guess was that he had dropped the receiver. Or thrown it down as he prepared to come.

''Thank you,'' she whispered to the silent night.

Soon Connor would be here. He would think she was inept. She moved to kneel behind Joey and he hunched away from her, as he stood up and went to stand looking out the window, poised to run or to watch for the only person he trusted. Alyssa didn't care what Connor thought.

She only hoped that he could do something.

But what could he do? He was a man who spent all his days with numbers and computers and machines. Cold. Judgmental.

What would he do when he was forced to deal with the demands of flesh and blood?

Four

As soon as his driver pulled up in front of Woodland Haven, Connor and Drifter were out the door and into the building.

"Thank you," Alyssa said, taking his coat. "I'm sorry for dragging you away from home, but I just couldn't leave him to tough out the night. It's obviously too soon for him to feel comfortable with me."

Her voice was soft. He had to give her credit for honesty. "Where is he?"

"In the playroom." She moved off, and he turned to head in that direction. He gave her more points for not offering to lead him there. Most people would have done that. Kind thoughts, but demeaning and unnecessary.

The echo of the floor changed as Connor moved down the hall and into the playroom. The scent of clay and paint and plastic from the children's toys filled his nostrils.

"Joey?" he called.

No answer at first. Then a faint, whispered "Here" sounded from across the room.

"Tough time sleeping tonight, huh?" Connor asked. "Happens to me, too."

No answer. No anything. Then a small sound. Movement.

"Yeah?" Joey asked, his voice barely registering in the silence.

"Definitely. How about you, Alyssa? Don't you ever have those nights?" The jasmine scent of her drifted in as she drew close.

He didn't know why he had included her. Maybe because she had humbled herself enough and trusted him enough to call him, even though it couldn't have been easy. Maybe because he would have been angry if he'd heard about this after the fact. Or maybe just because, as opposed to having her here as he was, he knew that it could only hurt the kids if she remained on the edge of their lives.

"More than you would believe," she admitted. "When I was a little girl and woke up unable to get back to sleep, I used to tell my folks that I'd heard an animal trying to get inside the house when really I just wanted to have someone to talk to. I doubt if they ever believed me, but it sounded good to me."

Joey grunted, though he didn't answer. Still, for a kid, a grunt could mean something. A start, Connor supposed.

"Boy, I can't sleep tonight either," Connor said.

"Must be one of those nights. I'm wide-awake," Alyssa agreed. "Wonder what we could do to pass the time."

No response from Joey.

"It's a long time until morning. We need something to do," Connor agreed.

"Till morning?" Joey's stilted, small voice squeaked in surprise.

"Could be. I could use a story or two, Joey. Maybe a game. How about you?"

"Who's reading?" It was a normal question, a typical kid question, and this time there was no fear or hesitation. Connor relaxed slightly, as much as he ever relaxed in the presence of others.

"I don't know who's reading. You?"

"Don't know enough words yet," Joey said.

"How about Alyssa?"

"How about you read and Joey and I will listen," she suggested. "You have a nice deep voice. If we're going to stay up all night, we need a voice that will keep us awake. Mine's too wimpy."

Hmmm, he had the feeling that she was manipulating him into reading because she didn't want him to have time to think about the fact that he had been called in like the cavalry. That was clever, not the work of a wimp, and there was nothing wimpy about her voice, either. Soft, yes. Husky, definitely. When she spoke, that voice crept in and made a man think of silk and fingers stroking on skin. He definitely did not want his thoughts going there, so yes, maybe she was right. He was the best choice to read, but he didn't like it. He never liked being the center of attention.

"You're sure you can't read?" he asked Joey.

"You do it."

"All right, go choose a book," he told the little boy, giving in. But when Joey had run off, Connor leaned close to Alyssa. "Payback time will come around, Alyssa."

"For calling you in the middle of the night?" Her soft voice, her scent drifted near. He could feel her heat and something else—desire?—which flowed through him, making his body feel tight and uncomfortable. Not good.

Surprising himself, he reached out and cupped her chin, the familiar jolt of awareness leaping almost out of control, so that he let go right away. "The payback won't be for waking me up." But he didn't explain. There were too many things about the woman that disturbed him, and not all of them were for sharing.

When Joey returned, he had a copy of *Saint George and the Dragon* in hand.

"One of my favorites," Alyssa said dreamily. Her tone made Connor frown. He didn't know if she was sincere or not, but she sounded much too feminine suddenly. He instantly wondered what she was wearing. It was, after all, the middle of the night.

But Joey had thrust the book into his hand, and there was nothing to do but sit down, place his fingers on the pages and read. He made sure that he was a good six feet away from Alyssa, though. He would have liked to offer to hold Joey on his lap, but he couldn't handle the book and the child, too.

"Would it be all right if you sat next to me?" he heard Alyssa whisper to Joey. "You don't have to."

"Whatever." He heard a small sound as the child scooted across the sofa.

"Thank you." Darn. That soft, naked voice again.

The book ended and Alyssa pulled out a Monopoly game, one made to be shared by the sighted and the blind.

"The night's still young," she said, and Connor held back a smile with great difficulty. He'd heard her trying to keep from yawning earlier. Most people wouldn't even have noticed. Probably Joey hadn't.

"We've got hours," Connor agreed. And the play began fast and furious. Or as fast as Monopoly ever was.

Connor played with less than half his attention. The rest was centered squarely on the woman across the board and the boy sitting to his right. When he sensed that Joey was beginning to finally relax, he bumped the board, sending the pieces scattering.

"Sorry," he apologized.

"You were probably going to win, anyway," Joey said. "The kids say that you try to let them win sometimes, but that never works."

"Lots of things don't work," Connor began slowly, struggling to find the right words. "Sometimes things you thought would be okay don't turn out the way you wanted. You know?"

"Yeah." The word was half-choked. Connor wondered if he should go on. And then he felt Alyssa's hand hovering over his arm. He jerked slightly before he caught himself.

"It's all right," he said, and she touched him. He felt it deep in his bones, the electricity again, the awareness, the startling sense that he knew things and could see things no person had a right to know and see about another. The sensations hit him in great waves as he struggled not to process the data, not to know the very essence of her. But he let none of that show. Instead he concentrated on finding the right words. That was the right path.

"You know I was raised at Woodland Haven?" he asked. "From birth?"

"Yes." Joey's answer was matter-of-fact, but Alyssa's fingers stiffened slightly. She hadn't known.

Connor smiled tightly. So much for maintaining a complete distance. He was sure someone had told her all there was to know. It could have been another barrier. And he could have warned her never to touch him, that she risked too much if she did. Well, it was too late for either of those things.

"The Haven was located in a different place back then, and when I was growing up there, twice people took me home with them. They meant well, I guess, but I wasn't an easy person to get along with, and my blindness turned out to be a problem for them, too. Both times I left the Haven smiling. Both times they brought me back disappointed. They said they felt bad, they hadn't meant to get my hopes up, but they told the director that it was better to find out things weren't going to work out sooner than later, wasn't it? Ticked me off royally, I'll tell you. Made me think things I didn't want to think."

For several seconds, Joey didn't say anything. Then he brushed against Connor. "They sure were stupid people, weren't they? Dumb, stupid, mean, ugly people. I hate them. I hate them to death."

Alyssa was clutching Connor's arm as if she was in shock. If she reprimanded Joey for saying he hated the people that had hurt him, things were going to get seriously complicated. Connor hated firing someone he'd just hired, especially when he'd promised her a month, but he had limits beyond which he couldn't go, and all too many child care workers concentrated too much on children never letting their honest feelings out. They thought that pretending not to feel the hateful things was better than ever letting the words slip through. He knew. Oh, yes. If Jane Barnette hadn't taken him under her wing and loved him so much and let him scream and yell and rant and rave and hate, really hate when he needed to, he didn't know how he would have survived those awful times.

"I don't know exactly how that feels." Alyssa's voice slid in low and gentle and hesitant. "I was already thirteen when my parents died and I went to the orphanage. Unattractive, awkward, sullen, thirteen-year-old girls are not very popular with prospective parents, so no one ever tried to adopt me. I would see them arrive and watch them look over the little ones, the cute ones, the cuddly ones. If they glanced my way at all, it was with a sense of dread, as if they were afraid someone would suggest that they take me home. Most looked right past me. I did hate them and began to make a point of appearing as ugly and angry as possible. I messed up my hair so that they would think I was mad. I wanted to scare them. If there was going to be some rejecting going on, I wanted to be the one to do it.

"Later, when I was older, I realized that I would have made some of those people happy. They didn't know who I was. They didn't take the time to know who I was. Those people who brought you back, Joey, they didn't get the chance to get to know you. They're missing out on this wonderful evening we're having here. It's their loss. Good riddance.''

Alyssa finished speaking and the silence filled in. She felt Connor's arm, warm and strong beneath her fingers, and she wanted to stroke it. The thought alarmed her. She pulled away.

Neither Connor nor Joey had spoken yet.

"Well, it's not exactly the same, I know," she said.

"Those people were bad," Joey said suddenly.

"Not bad, just ignorant, uninformed, scared," she told him.

Connor still hadn't spoken, but she knew she had his full attention. Probably he was wondering why she hadn't volunteered the fact that she had lived in an orphanage. It hadn't been on her résumé. Of course it hadn't.

"Do you think anyone will ever adopt me?" Joey said, his voice small and squeaky.

She wanted to rush in and say, "Oh yes, baby, of course they will," or "Don't worry, sweetheart, you'll find the right parents."

"I don't know," she and Connor answered in unison, their voices joining like lovers. "You first," she said to Connor.

He gave her a half smile. "I can't predict the future, Joey, but you'll always have a home here. I'll always be here for you. It's the best I can offer you."

Alyssa felt her throat closing. She wanted to make the little boy a promise, too, but that would have been wrong. Her own future here was uncertain.

"Are you okay enough to sleep now?" she asked gently, daring to touch Joey's dark curls.

He stiffened slightly beneath her fingers but didn't pull away. "Yeah. Bud and David are sure going to be jealous when they hear that I got to stay up late," he said.

She chuckled. "Don't tease them, okay?"

"'kay."

"Come on, then. We'll get you to bed."

But Joey turned to look at Connor. "You come, too."

"Try and stop me."

Alyssa had the feeling that not many people tried to stop Connor from doing what he wanted. But as she moved toward the dark bedroom alone with him and Joey, the situation felt too intimate. "Good night, Joey," she said at the door.

"Night." He turned and gave her a tiny, tight, macho smile. She wanted to hug him, but she was pretty sure he wasn't ready for that. Maybe he never would be. Not everyone felt comfortable with hugs.

She watched Connor follow Joey to the bed. He reached down and awkwardly tucked the little boy in. "Good night, son," he said.

"G'night." And Joey turned over and relaxed into the pillow. He was already half-asleep.

Connor, however, seemed completely alert when he turned from the bed and walked toward her.

"Let's go downstairs to my office," she whispered. "Maybe I'll apologize for keeping secrets about my past."

"Maybe you'll tell me who you really are." He followed her back to the darkened room.

She reached for the light switch, but before she could flip it on, Connor touched her sleeve, his hand stilling her movement. "Tell me why you never mentioned the orphanage."

"Why should I have?"

"Maybe I would have been easier on you."

"Would you have?"

"No, but most people would have thought I would have."

"Maybe that's why I didn't. Spending my teen years in an orphanage was beyond my control. I had no hand in it. There was no accomplishment in it. I like to make my way on my own."

"You have things to prove."

"Don't you?"

He didn't answer at first. "No," he finally said. "Nothing to prove."

"But I am sorry."

"Because you lied to me."

"I didn't."

"Yes, a sin of omission is still a sin. In a job such as this, it's important to lay all your cards on the table. Anything that might help the children matters."

"I hadn't thought of it that way."

"Next time think that way. So why are you sorry?"

"I got you out of bed."

"Yes."

"I didn't handle the situation on my own."

"You said that Joey was inconsolable. Scared. Crying out."

"He was, but I can't count on you running to the rescue all the time. I'm the director here. I should have been able to handle it. Perhaps I should have—"

And suddenly his hands were on her face. She gazed

up at him in the dark and felt him slide his fingers down, touching her brows, her nose, her lips, then cupping her jaw in his palms.

"You did handle it. You called me."

"Now that he's more calm, it seems like it was a cowardly thing to do."

"It was the right thing to do." He kissed her, his lips like warm velvet on hers. They stroked her, tempted her and made her ache, then move away.

"Now, that?" he said, "that was the wrong thing to do. Now you know the difference. If it's personal, you and me, it's wrong. If it pertains to the kids, no matter what, no matter what hour, what the weather, no matter where I am or what I'm doing, you call me. I'll come. That's the right thing. That's the only thing."

Then he called to Drifter, took the handle of the dog's harness and swept out the door.

Alyssa watched him move out into the night and into the waiting car. She touched her lips. What kind of man was Connor Quinn?

Her lips ached, they itched, they burned with yearning.

What kind of man? A man who was kind to children. Beyond that she didn't want to know.

A foundling home, Jake thought. How many were there in the country? And how many had received baby boys in the year 1967? Obviously, a great many. But how many of those babies had been blind?

"More than you'd think," he muttered. The information was proving more difficult to dig up than he'd anticipated. The directors of the facilities had a tendency to be more closemouthed than any secret intelligence officer he'd ever encountered.

And why not? These were children they were dealing with. Innocents. His brother had been an innocent. He'd probably grown up completely ignorant of the fact that he'd even had a family somewhere.

Probably best to leave things that way, Jake thought. It wasn't as if he didn't have enough other things to keep him busy. Achilles was still on the loose, still no closer to being found. And maybe he was preparing to strike again if Jake didn't find him soon. The case was taking up all his days and nights, and that wasn't sitting well with Tara, because he couldn't even tell her what he was doing.

He recalled the last tantrum his fiancée had indulged in, if you could call it a tantrum. More like chilling him to the bone. He knew he should share something more of himself and his situation with her, but…

"Not yet," he murmured. "Not yet."

His responsibilities were pressing down on him and they *were* his responsibilities. Gideon was at large somewhere. Did Gideon know about his blind brother? If he did and if he or the Coalition found his missing sibling, what would they tell him? Would they let him know that there were others like him? Would they offer to link him with his family for a price? And what might a man with those kinds of abilities be capable of if he was offered the right bait?

The Coalition had used Gideon to mastermind the World Bank Heist. What if they now had two men like Gideon?

And what was the right bait?

"Family," Jake said again. A man raised in an orphanage with superhuman mental capabilities would stand alone. He'd crave the stimulation of others like himself. Gideon and the Coalition could offer him that.

"But not if I get to him first," Jake swore, and he swept all thoughts of Tara out of his mind. If he worked very hard and fast, he could whittle down this list in no time at all.

His brother was out there. It was up to Jake to find him before someone else did.

Five

"Mr. Quinn is here," Edwina told Alyssa some days later. "Just thought you might want to know. The two of you seem to be like two high-strung wild animals around each other."

"An interesting observation, Edwina," Alyssa said, looking up from the papers she was perusing. A couple was due to come for a visit later today. They'd been through all the paperwork and preliminary procedures and had passed all the tests. Now came the real test, dealing with the children. The thought made Alyssa edgy. "What's Connor here for this time? Did he discover that I didn't declare that my left incisor has been capped and I didn't list it on my résumé?"

Edwina's eyebrows rose. "Well, I...I truly don't know. He's just here. He just comes by now and then. I don't ask him his reasons. He's our benefactor, after all, and—"

Alyssa held up one hand and smiled. "I'm just kidding, Edwina."

"Besides, Alyssa knows that I came by to see if she was going to drag out her dirty laundry." Connor's dry voice slipped into the room, and Alyssa looked up to see him standing in the doorway. He gave Drifter permission to lie down and leaned his shoulder against the door frame. "Left incisor, did you say? I'll have to make a note of it."

Alyssa was glad Connor couldn't tell that she was blushing. Or maybe he could. The man didn't miss much, and he would certainly be the type to note that she was practically squirming in her seat. What was almost soundless to her was instantly noticeable to him.

Heat flooded her body as she remembered that the last time she'd seen him, his lips had been against hers. Had she responded? Had he noticed? Please, no. His kiss had been a warning, only that. He had definitely made it clear that he wasn't interested.

Well, she wasn't interested, either. She wanted a man, but not a man like Connor. What she wanted was an ordinary man, someone who would finally see her for herself and who would want to settle down with her and raise babies. Connor Quinn didn't qualify as ordinary in any way.

And if she didn't say something soon, he'd think she was remembering that kiss.

"Well, I'll just leap right in and modify my employee record immediately," she quipped, rising from her chair and moving around her desk. "So, what really does bring you to Woodland Haven today, may I ask? I wouldn't have thought most benefactors of your ilk spent this much time with the recipients of their largesse."

Edwina muttered a quick "I'll just be leaving," and Connor stepped aside to let her pass.

Connor tipped Alyssa a nod. "Most benefactors probably don't, but you know that my history with the

Haven goes back. This was my home. I was one of these kids. I stop in a lot. Get used to it.''

As if anyone could ever get used to having this man around. He took up space, he stole her wit, he put her on the defensive. And she was far too aware of him as a man. Wouldn't do at all.

She fiddled with her watch. "All right. You want the details of how each week goes?''

"It's not a requirement.''

"But it would ease your mind.''

He dragged in a breath. Okay, nothing was going to ease his mind. He saw her as a piece of high-fashion fluff. She dreaded telling him what she'd been up to this week.

"I've made some tentative changes to the program here.''

"Such as?''

"Setting up a teen night on Fridays where they can go out and be with other kids.''

"Separating them from the younger ones? That's not our way.''

"They need time alone.''

"Everyone here is family.''

"I'm not denying that, but they're teenagers. They need to have their own time. They're different.''

His expression turned thunderous. "Different." The word sounded like a curse.

"It's not a dirty word.''

"Separating them will make them feel awkward and self-conscious.''

"It's not a mandatory separation. Those who choose to stay with the group for Friday-night movies or board games can do so. The ones who want a separate pizza party or to play cards on their own can do that, too. I'm also bringing in a few experts to talk to them about issues that pertain to teenagers, including those who know something about the social issues that affect teenagers growing up in orphanages."

"The counselors already do that."

"Yes, but these will be experts."

"Our counselors are experts."

"People who've had the same experiences," she clarified. "Recently. College kids."

"Kids?"

Alyssa couldn't keep from chuckling. "Let's try it. I'll keep my eyes open for problem areas. I'll let the children here give me feedback on whether it's helping or hurting them. I want them to have more of a hand in what happens to them. They're growing up. They need this kind of thing. At least, in my opinion, they do," she couldn't help but add.

He moved a step closer. "In other words, you don't know for sure."

"No."

"You've never done this before."

"You know I haven't. You've read my résumé."

"Ah, the résumé. That again."

"Yes."

"You want to change things."

"You brought me here to direct."

"I didn't bring you here."

"You're right, but you let me stay on a trial basis. Well, I'm running a trial program for the teens. If it fails, we pitch it, just as you'll pitch me if I fail. Is that fair?''

"I think so. Except…are you doing this to prove something?"

"I'm doing this because I was a teenager in an orphanage once, and I needed things that weren't provided for me. I'm trying to make sure that doesn't happen to our kids."

"So you're doing this as a reaction to the way you were raised?"

"Aren't you?"

He turned more fully toward her. "What do you mean?"

"Isn't the very fact that you're the benefactor of the Haven a reaction to the way you were raised? Something must have made you want to help the children here."

"Yes, but it wasn't a bad thing. I had a wonderful director who took me under her wing and raised me like a son."

"So you were happy here."

"I was what I was."

She chuckled. "That's certainly telling me to mind my own business in no uncertain terms."

"I'm a blunt man, Alyssa."

"You're in a position to be a blunt man."

"And you're a blunt woman."

"So I've been told."

"By men?"

Now it was her turn to hesitate.

"I'd say the answer was yes," he said softly. "Mind if I ask what you told the man?"

"I told him what I thought of him."

He laughed, a low, rough, sexy sound. "What did he do that made you think badly of him?"

She hesitated. "He asked me to marry him."

That stopped him cold. For all of three seconds. "You didn't want to marry him, I take it." His voice grew even rougher.

"I— No. He definitely wasn't the right man for me."

"And the right man would be?"

"Ordinary. Very ordinary, and he would want children."

Something unreadable, almost frightening, turned Connor's expression to granite. "Children. I see. I take it this man didn't want them. It isn't a sin, you know. Some men have good reasons."

"I'm sure they do, and I don't fault them. I just don't want to marry one. I'm sure you understand. You'll undoubtedly want children when you marry."

"I won't want to marry, and if I ever did, I wouldn't have children."

Her heart stopped beating, or so it seemed. His words were so cold, so chilling, so certain. For a second she thought she heard anguish in his voice, but his face was impassive. He had those darn dark glasses on again, a mask that made his features unreadable.

"But you love children." Her voice sounded like a child's. She hated the fact that he had opened a chink in her own armor.

Connor smiled, a bitter smile. "Take care of mine, Alyssa. And damn it, let me know how your experiment works. Next time, though, let me know when you intend to institute major changes."

She took a deep breath. "Yes, I will."

"So you intend to make more changes?"

"Yes."

"Why?"

"Some change, a small change now and then, makes us stop and reassess what we're doing. It keeps us feeling alive. But I'll definitely speak to you first. I won't do anything until then."

The truth was that she didn't even have any specific changes in mind for now. She had a terrible feeling that she'd enjoy simply thinking up new and outrageous plans just so she could spar with Connor over them. The man put her on the defensive, and for some reason she couldn't fathom and didn't want to examine, he made her feel something else.

Exhilaration.

He made her heart trip along faster. That wasn't good. If she wanted to make her heart beat faster, she should take up jogging and leave Connor to his mathematical formulas and his isolated life.

Or was it isolated?

Just because he didn't plan to marry didn't mean he didn't have women.

The thought made her angry. It made her want to scream.

She'd been feeling like screaming ever since she'd met Connor Quinn. Maybe he was right; maybe she didn't belong here, and perhaps she should just bow out now.

While she was still safe.

"I went over to the Haven to help with the new sound system." Connor's business associate Tom Winters made the comment a bit too casually, and Connor lifted his fingers from his computer keyboard and leaned back in his chair. It had been two days since Connor's conversation with Alyssa.

"And your point is…"

"I saw Alyssa Fielding." Tom let out a low wolf whistle. "Man, if I had gotten to look at legs of that caliber every day when I was a teenage boy, I would have spent all my days and nights fantasizing."

"Which you're obviously not doing right now." Connor couldn't quite keep the acidity from his voice. Tom Winters was a mathematical whiz kid, but he also considered himself to be a ladies' man. Obviously, he was targeting Alyssa.

"Hell, yes, I am. Nothing wrong with a little fantasy. And when you're talking about a blond beauty with huge blue eyes and a neck made for a man's lips…" Tom made a sound that could only be him smacking his own lips.

Connor barely restrained himself from asking Tom to leave the room.

"Oh, yeah. I have to agree with the man," Brian Lester said, his voice growing louder as he entered the room. "I saw her, too. She definitely goes on my list of the five most beautiful women in the area." Brian was always making lists. This was his favorite. "Great breasts, too, you know?"

Heat rose in Connor's chest. Of course he didn't know.

"High and round, about the size of grapefruit, the pale-pink kind."

Brian was forever trying to be helpful in his descriptions. There were times when he was simply amusing, but today Connor just wasn't amused.

"That'll be enough," he said. "Alyssa Fielding is the director of Woodland Haven. As such, she's under my protection."

"Hey, I respect the woman completely," Tom said earnestly.

And if he thought he had the least chance with her, he would be over there trying to talk her into his bed. Connor knew the man.

"If you respect her, you'll lay off discussing her legs or her neck. Or her breasts," Connor said, pointedly turning toward Brian. "The lady is off-limits to any Solutions Unlimited employees. Got that?"

"I knew that," Brian said. "But a man can dream, can't he? A woman who looks like that only enters a guy's world a couple of times in his life. Wouldn't be natural to look and not imagine what a night in her bed would be like, would it?"

"Don't make me regret that I hired you, Lester," Connor said.

"You know I'm the best, Connor."

He was. But right now he was not high on Connor's list of favorite people. And not just because Brian was a lecherous worm, Connor thought as the two men took off for lunch. But because, for the first time in a long time, they'd made Connor regret that he didn't have the ability to experience what they experienced.

He hated feeling like that.

It had been years since he'd allowed himself to even think that way. Not since he'd been engaged to Lynnette. He'd had his share of women since then, some reputedly beautiful, but none that had made him wish for things that couldn't be.

But damn Alyssa's apparently gorgeous eyes and womanly breasts and his men's big mouths.

He was doing it again—wishing he could see what it was that caused men to act like teenage boys when she was around. Not that he wanted to know. He didn't want Alyssa Fielding fueling his nighttime fantasies.

At least, he didn't want her fueling them more than she already was. Ever since he'd touched her, with all that soft, scented skin and those moist, full lips, his nights had been restless.

No more. For the next few days, at least until he had learned to smother his reaction to Alyssa, he was going to keep his distance from Woodland Haven. The project was far enough along that his men could handle the detail work.

Of course, he was going to send out a directive that no one, absolutely no one, was to mess with the Haven's director. He didn't want her to feel uncomfortable because his employees were ogling her.

If he could control his reactions to Alyssa, then damn it, his men could, too. He was not going near her for a while.

"Agnes, it's been too quiet lately," Dr. Oliver Grimble said to his partner.

"I'm not worried," Agnes Payne told him. "We spent years doing our homework and building the Coalition. Jake Ingram and his three siblings may be geniuses, but they don't know exactly what they're looking for. They don't know what we know. And they don't have Achilles.''

''I'd feel better, though, if we could put a stop to Ingram and what he's doing. I need to know what he's up to right now.''

''You know that we've tried repeatedly to get close. He and his are always guarded. What we need is someone close to him that he's overlooked, someone he isn't providing protection for. Then we hold the key to Jake and the rest of the Proteans.''

''So let's find someone.''

''Oh, we will. Believe me, we will. And when we do, we'll send a message. Anyone who gets in our way will face elimination. To paraphrase a cliché, my dear partner, you either work against us, or you work for us. If we find the right person, someone close to Jake Ingram, who'll work for us, that will be a coup. We already have Gideon. We haven't been lucky enough to get hold of Ingram's other siblings, and his fiancée is protected, but surely there's one person he's overlooked, someone we can get to, someone we can make use of.''

''And if that person cannot be used?''

''Everyone can be used. Everyone has a weakness, some thing or some persons they treasure. All we have to do is find the weakness.''

Agnes's smile was terrible to behold. She and Oliver had waited years for their work to come to fruition. No mere mortal was going to stop them now.

Of course, Jake was no mere mortal and neither were his brothers and sisters, but all of the genetically engineered babies had been accounted for now. Anyone else that was close to Jake would be easy to manipulate, just another ordinary human.

Connor woke from sleep and realized that he was fully aroused. No need to wonder what it was that had sent him into such a state. He could still smell the scent of jasmine, even though he hadn't seen her in several days. And thanks to his damned colleagues' descriptions of the length of her legs and his own foolhardiness in touching her the other day, he could feel her beneath his fingertips.

"Damn it to hell," he said, shoving back the blankets and rising nude from his bed. For several moments he just stood there, sensing every ion of the building, just as he had been able to "see" Alyssa's life force the other day when his fingers had rested on her skin. It was this sense of inner vision as much as his blindness that set him apart from other men. It had aided him immensely in his inventions and helped make him rich, but it also made him different, and it made people fear him when they suspected. Even Jane Barnette had been spooked, and she had raised him from birth and loved him.

He wondered if Alyssa had felt how different his touch had been from other men's touches. He hoped he hadn't frightened her. But it didn't matter in the long run. He wasn't going to touch her again. He couldn't control his dreams, but surely he could control his actions.

Because the fact remained that he wasn't an ordinary man. He never had been and never would be. And no amount of wishing he could claim the type of life that other men claimed would change things.

There were definite barriers to touching Alyssa, and the least of those was that he was her employer.

"So you're never going to touch those long legs or taste those bountiful breasts, Quinn," he told himself in a rough voice. "Dream on if you can't help it, but make sure you don't get too near. She's not going to know just what you are, because you aren't going to let your powers near her again."

Six

The phone rang in his office a few days later, and Connor automatically picked it up.

"Mr. Quinn?" The voice on the other end of the line was that of a female, someone in her midtwenties he'd guess.

"Yes, this is Quinn. And you would be...?"

"I work at the Haven. I think you'd better get over here right away."

"Is someone sick? Hurt? Some problem at the building site?"

"It's that woman."

Connor drew back from the phone at the venom in the young woman's voice.

"Which woman?" he asked, his voice turning cool and expressionless.

"Ms. Fielding. The one you didn't want to hire."

He noted the comment. This wasn't anyone he had encountered at the school in his recent visits with Alyssa. Edwina, the head teacher, and Nola, the housemother, had both seemed to love her.

"And what seems to be the problem with Ms. Fielding?" he asked cautiously.

"There are reporters here, to talk to her and take pictures. It's not the first time, either."

Instantly, Connor's cool demeanor turned volcanic. The woman had brought reporters into the midst of a group of sensitive children, some of whom might be considered interestingly freakish to a certain element in the world. If a magazine gained entrance to the Haven, the orphanage and its inhabitants would be turned into a circus sideshow.

And there would be scores of pictures of Alyssa all over the tabloids. More men like Tom and Brian drooling over her and mentally measuring the length of her legs or imagining how her bare breasts would feel against their bodies.

Not that he should care that men thought of her that way. But he did.

He pushed a button on his intercom system. "Jerry, bring my car around. Come, Drifter," he said, rising from his chair. "Forward."

It wasn't until he was almost at the school that he realized he had left the young caller hanging on the line.

It was starting to snow harder than it had been an hour ago, Alyssa thought, gazing out the oversize window into the gathering darkness as the flakes drifted down like soft white feathers. The children would have loved to be out in this, she thought. And she would have allowed them to, but Mrs. Engels, the literature teacher, was staging a play, and the children were all being given parts today. Every last one of them. She was going to have to be creative in coming up with enough people to make up an audience. The kids would be disappointed if they didn't have someone to watch their efforts.

Alyssa was just starting to mentally tally the number of old friends she could call, who in turn could call more friends, when Connor's black limo pulled up in the drive. The car was struggling with the several inches of snow that already made the long, unplowed drive slippery.

"What on earth can the man want now?" she whispered, standing at her office window. "And why would he make that long drive from his office in this mess? Maybe he came to see if I failed to include something else on my résumé," she joked.

But one look at Connor's stormy expression when he and Drifter exited the limo sent all traces of humor fluttering away like the snowflakes. He had left his glasses off. That could only mean one thing where she was concerned. And the limo was leaving. Obviously, Connor intended to stay awhile.

The man was incensed about something, and he meant to intimidate.

"Well, let's get this over with," Alyssa said, moving to the door. But before she could open it, it flew back.

She blinked. "Well, come in, Connor. Just out for a little jaunt in the snow?" she asked, her voice tinged with ice.

"Snow?"

"The stuff you're wading through."

She moved behind her desk, prepared to be polite if she had to force every word out and to offer Connor coffee like a good hostess. But he closed the door behind them with a rough click, then turned and rounded her desk, crowding her.

"I know what snow is and what it feels like." He

clipped the words off. "What I want to know is where the reporters are. Who are they taking pictures of and what do they intend to write? And for the record, Ms. Fielding, I thought I made myself clear from day one that I did not want you to mix your former career showing off your skin with my children."

She couldn't help the gasp. So that was what this was about. "You have a lot of nerve, Connor, and I have to tell you that you're treading on thin ice here."

"Do you deny that there are reporters here?"

"Yes."

"So there are no reporters here."

"Not anymore."

"But they were here." She didn't care how gorgeous and talented he was and how good he was with Joey and how his touch had felt. She didn't even care how dedicated he was to the children of the Haven. Not right now. For now all she could manage to register was the fact that, once again, she was being judged based on appearances.

"Yes, they were here and I posed naked for them," she said. "Are you happy now? Yes, my true colors did finally show through, and I couldn't help myself. I had to be in the camera's spotlight. It's my nature, after all, Connor, and I can't fight it."

Dark color was climbing from the collar of his white shirt. He stepped forward and reached out.

He was close, so close, and if his hand continued on in that path, he was going to brush her breast. No doubt he would assume that she had moved so that he would not make full contact with her. She probably should slide away so that she could avoid his touch altogether.

Instead, she stepped forward, right into the path of his fingers. As his skin just grazed the side of her breast, dark heat enveloped her. It was just the way it had been when he'd touched her before, as if a part of herself she hadn't known even existed opened and unfolded for him. It was as if she had been bared to all his senses, as if she couldn't help but reveal her innermost secrets to him.

She remembered now what she'd tried to forget, that when he'd touched her she had wanted to lean closer, to ask him to linger, to touch more.

A mistake, she thought, trying to control her thoughts and her reactions to the man. Quickly she started to step back, but no. That would be to admit that he had the upper hand here.

"See?" she said, trying to keep her voice from wobbling. "I crave attention in any way I can get it."

For a moment, just a whisper of a second, his fingers flexed and his index finger caressed the curve of her breast.

Her flesh tightened. She longed to press closer.

And then he pulled back.

"I see," he said. "But you didn't answer my question. Where are they?" His voice was a soft stroke of sound now. Coaxing, demanding.

"They're gone. They got what they came for."

"Nude pictures of you."

"Yes."

"Um, I see." He reached out again, and touched one finger to the side of her neck. Her heartbeat began to thunder in her ears. "That's all they wanted. You naked."

"Yes."

"And you obliged them."

"Of course. I'm a professional exhibitionist."

Suddenly he lifted his lips in a trace of a smile. "I hope you're a better exhibitionist than you are a liar."

"What...what do you mean?"

He stroked her neck again. "I mean that for a woman who's used to shedding all of her clothes in front an entire crew of men, you shiver too much when one man touches you."

"I...I don't even think about the cameramen. It's not the same."

He drew his hand away. "Perhaps you're right. It's not the same. So tell me, Alyssa, just where were the children when all of this was going on?"

That was it. She had had enough. Her breast was aching and her neck was aching, and she had a very bad feeling that the ache signified need, not pain or fear or disgust. And that was so unfair, that she wanted him to touch her while all he wanted was to humiliate her and get rid of her. Besides, there was something else bothering her.

She stepped forward right up against him, ignoring the sensations that caused. "What is wrong with you? What kind of man are you, anyway? Do you really think that I'd let reporters in here to take advantage of my kids? Do you think I'd let them take photos of my children and let them plaster their faces all over the pages of a glossy magazine? Do you know what an invitation that would be to the perverts and lowlifes of the world? A bunch of needy kids who want parents. Do you know what kind of people that would bring out of the woodwork? And I would be doing this for what reason? Because I'm so self-centered and egotistical and narcissistic and totally stupid that I just couldn't help myself? What kind of woman do you think I am, anyway? No, don't even answer that. You've already made it clear that you know my type."

She stopped speaking. Her lips were only inches from his chest. Hot tears pressed against the backs of her eyelids. Well, what kind of woman cried just because she faced a little adversity? Maybe she didn't deserve to work with these children.

"Alyssa." His voice was low, softer than she'd ever heard it.

She shook her head, her hair brushing his chest as she leaned. "Don't say another word."

"I have to."

"You've said enough."

"Too much," he agreed. "I don't think you're stupid. I never thought that. How could I? After all, I've read your résumé." His words teased, but his voice was raw. He held his hands out as if he would wrap his arms around her, but he didn't touch. "I'm the stupid one," he said.

A hollow laugh slipped through her lips. "Oh, that's rich, Connor. You're a genius. Everyone knows that."

"Am I now? Am I really?" And there was something low in his voice that mocked himself, that called to her, that made her want to rake *her* fingers across him.

She backed away slightly.

He smiled and began to circle her slowly.

"So what did you do with them?"

"Who?"

"The reporters? Did you tie them up and stuff them in a closet? Did you take one of the cook's butter knives and fend them off?"

Connor heard Alyssa drag in a deep breath. She was wary of him now, angry and sad and very, very nervous. That one breath said it all. The fact that she was fidgeting once again said more. He'd noticed her nervous tendency to fuss with her clothing. The smoothing sounds of hands over cloth were unmistakable. And maybe it was just a former model's subconscious tendency to make everything look perfect, or maybe it was something more, deeper, something very human and endearing.

He shouldn't have touched her. He definitely shouldn't have done that, but he didn't regret it. Not for a minute. She was heaven to touch.

But more than that, she was magnificent in her anger. He'd come to her on the say-so of an anonymous voice on the phone, someone who clearly had an ax to grind. He'd worked with his share of the same kind of vindictive person over the years, but he had judged Alyssa based on that telephone voice. Because she scared him. Because she terrified him. Because he wanted her.

"There *were* reporters?" he asked, at her back now. God, the way she had stood up to him! He knew he was a big man, an intimidating man, and he had committed the ultimate sin for him. He had touched her, allowed her to feel his power, and still she had moved into him, challenged him. As grumpy and wrong as he had been, she had been awe inspiring.

He heard her take a calming breath. He'd just bet that she was squaring her shoulders and lifting her chin.

"There were reporters," she finally admitted.

"And where are they now?"

She shifted, the sound of her clothing sliding. "Gone back to where they came from, just as all the rest have. I sent them away, of course."

"There have been others?"

She leaned closer. "Dozens."

He could see she was gearing up again, getting angry again, preparing to tell him that she'd stripped her clothes off for a group of anonymous men and readers. The thought of her naked hit him again, and he nearly lost his breath. He struggled to blot out the sensations.

"Guess I've been pretty ignorant," he said.

And suddenly she laughed, just a tiny thing, but, oh, it was a lovely sound. "You've been very ignorant," she agreed. "But for a very good cause. They matter to me, you know. The kids."

"I think I'm beginning to know."

"They matter so much. I would never betray them, Connor, and for the record, I have no interest in appearing before the cameras ever again. It was a job while I held it, and it helped pay the bills and get me through college. Yes, it was a bit exciting, but it's in my past. There *have* been reporters and there will be more. I guess I was somewhat cowardly in not letting you know earlier. Maybe because you predicted it would happen, and I didn't want you to win. How did you know they were here, anyway?"

"An anonymous phone call from the school."

"Oh." Her voice was too calm, her distress evident.

"I'll find out who it was and have them dismissed."

"No," she said very quickly. "It's up to me to win

over my employees and fight my battles. I'll explain the reporter situation to the staff and make sure that everyone understands.''

''Sometimes you have to let people go, Alyssa.'' He knew what she was thinking. He had almost let *her* go.

''I know that,'' she said. ''And if someone has to be dismissed, I'm up to it. But not without giving that person a chance. You gave me one.''

He nodded. ''But you can't forgive me for the fact that I did it reluctantly.''

''I can understand. Maybe that's why I didn't tell you about the reporters. I didn't want to leave.''

''That's good. You're obviously having a positive effect. Edwina tells me the new teen program is making David and Wendy and the others come alive.''

''You checked up on me?''

''Yes. Did you think I wouldn't?''

''I guess I thought… Well, I knew you would. I just haven't seen you for the past couple of days. There were reporters here yesterday, too. I yelled at them,'' she confided. ''I threatened to call the police if they didn't leave. Then I threatened to call you. That did the trick.''

He couldn't help himself then. She seemed so pleased with herself, so utterly unaware of how enticing she was, that he reached out.

''I don't think that's a good idea,'' she said.

''I do,'' he answered as he heard her scurrying away. How could he tell her that he'd touched these walls, he knew every molecule of this room. He could feel where she was.

A soft knock sounded on the door. He barely registered the sound.

"It's Mrs. Morrissey," a voice called when he answered. "Are you in there, Ms. Fielding?"

"Yes." Alyssa's voice was shaky.

"All right, then. The teachers have already departed, dear. I've left young Wendy in charge, and I'm going now. Are you sure you'll be all right here alone tonight?"

"We'll be just fine. Tell your sister I hope she's feeling better."

"I will," and the sound of Nola's shoes sounded as she headed for the back entrance.

"Her sister?"

"Has the flu. She lives on the property, you know. You were the one who told her she could stay," Alyssa reminded him.

"I guess I did."

"You're not as bad as you make yourself out to be," she said softly.

"Oh, yes, I am." And to prove it, he reached out and took her hand. With his other hand, he touched her palm, his fingers sliding over the surface, learning her, feeling her heat, feeling her. He traced the outline of each finger, raked his thumb over each nail, touched each joint and then returned to the sensitive skin of her palm. Stroking, gorging on her, learning her. Leaving heat licking at his senses.

She froze. "Wh-what are you doing?"

"Touching you."

"Just touching me? I don't think you should. I don't believe you and I should get that intense."

Her voice was as thin as breath could make it. There

was awareness there, desire, but also something else. Fear. He knew the sound; he'd heard it before.

Immediately he let go of her hand.

Deep, hot anger filled him. He'd known what he'd been doing. He knew that when he touched a woman he was doing more than touching her. His inner vision made him more aware of her body than another man would be. So, touching her hand was much more significant than it would be for any other man. In touching her, he took advantage, he violated her, especially since she was unaware of what this simple exchange meant.

And she should know. It was the solution, after all. If she knew, she would know what he was. She would fear him more. It would create a safe distance, and that was what he wanted, wasn't it? To create a distance, to stop wanting her, stop wanting the impossible.

"You're right," he said softly. "I shouldn't touch you. I'm not like other men, and not just because of my skills with math and technology. I don't see with my eyes, Alyssa, but I see more. When I touch just this soft place here on you," he said, indicating his own palm, "I feel the throbbing of your blood, the beating of your heart. I sense the quickening of your breath, even if it's too soft to hear. And I'm aware of every detail of the very contours of your body."

She jumped, and he felt it as her shoes slipped and she nearly stumbled. He reached out to catch her, and she stepped back slightly. His hand skimmed her arm, just to make sure she didn't slip, but the contact was enough. Heat seared through him. He "saw" her, he wanted her, and she was aware as she hadn't been before. Now she knew, now she was afraid of him. "Connor, I—"

He reached out to stop her by placing his fingers on her lips, but he stopped just shy of her mouth, her breath warm against his fingertips.

"You're right. I shouldn't have touched you, certainly not without your consent. I know what I am and what a violation that is, so touching you was... Well, it's not the kind of thing I'm proud of. And yes, it's best if you and I don't get too intense. I should leave."

He heard her take in a deep breath, deeper than usual. She whirled away, walked away.

"I don't believe that's going to be possible," she said faintly.

"Why is that?"

"The snow. It's become very deep. And your car isn't here."

"I'll call Jerry."

But when he hung up the phone seconds later, Connor was frowning. "You're right. The snow is too deep for Jerry to get back in here safely. The road outside the school is closed until the plows get through, and the plows are working to get the main roads cleared."

"Looks like you're stuck here with me and the children, Connor. Welcome home to the Haven." But Connor noticed that her voice shook as she said the words.

"I've found him. It has to be him," Jake told his sister, Gretchen.

Gretchen, like Jake and their missing brother, was one of the original siblings in their father's experiment, and they shared an unbreakable bond. A cryptologist without equal, she and her husband, Kurt, were expecting their first child. They lived off the coast of Portugal on the island of Brunhia, but Jake visited as much as he could. Gretchen understood like no other Jake's deep personal need to find his brother who had shared their mother's womb.

"Are you sure?"

"As sure as I can be. He's at Woodland Haven in Boston. It's a foundling home, and a baby named Connor Quinn was taken there back in 1967. He was blind from birth. Now he's grown and he runs a company called Solutions Unlimited that creates amazingly intricate devices to make people's lives easier. Some say his inventions are unexplainable."

"So you think the programming took, after all."

"Seems likely."

"That makes him one of us."

"It also makes him potentially dangerous if the Coalition gets to him before we do."

"So let's get him, Jake."

"I can't. A major snowstorm around Boston has mucked up communications. His home lines are down, his company lines are down, Woodland Haven's lines are down, and though I was able to ferret out a cell phone number, he must have turned it off. Looks like I'll have to wait until either the phones are working or the roads are clear."

"You're thinking of going to Boston?"

"If it's him, I'm definitely going to Boston."

"Does Tara know?"

He hesitated. "Not yet. And yes, I know, a man shouldn't keep such secrets from his fiancée. The thing is, Gretchen, that I want to tell her. Hell, I want to tell her everything, but not yet. It's not the right time. And besides, she's safer this way.'' He knew that his words sounded hollow. They sounded hollow even to himself. He couldn't figure out why he was keeping all the most important things about himself from Tara, but...

"I'll tell her eventually,'' he promised.

"You want me to call her and tell her you got called away on business unexpectedly?'' she offered. Warmth flooded Jake's soul. He'd missed his family and hadn't even known it. Regret coursed through him that none of them had even known the others existed until now. And now there was one more.

"Thanks, but no. I'll call her before I leave and tell her something. It can't be the truth.'' He hated that. There had been nothing but lies between him and Tara for what seemed like forever. She'd been bitter lately, angry. There were times he thought that she hated him, and who could blame her?

"Do you think the Coalition knows about Connor?'' Gretchen asked.

"I don't know. I hope not, but I can't take that chance. I have to reach him before they do.''

"Be careful. If they've gotten there before us, and Connor is one of us, you may not be able to bring him into the family.''

"It may be more complicated than that.''

"What do you mean?''

"Word on the street is that Connor Quinn is a loner and wants to keep it that way. He may not want to become a member of our family or any other.''

Seven

He'd never stayed overnight at the school, at least not since he'd grown to manhood, and certainly not since he'd moved the school to the countryside outside of Boston. Even though this had been his home as a boy, legions of children and teachers had come and gone since then, and now all that remained of *his* Woodland Haven was the history.

Even the building was new, but when he'd moved the Haven here, he'd made a point of learning the structure just as well as he did his home and office. He knew the Haven inside and out, upside down and right side out. He could find his way through the rooms without even having Drifter to guide him.

But a meal at a table set in an unfamiliar manner, with dishes whose whereabouts eluded him, could be a nightmare. It could bring back all the old insecurities, the memories of people or at least one person, making him realize how different he was, how much of a burden, how unacceptable.

"Connor, you'll take the head of the table tonight, won't you?" Alyssa's cool gentle voice flowed through him. "That way all the children will be able to see you and talk to you."

It was her place to take the head of the table. He

almost said so, but then he felt her breath warm on his ear. Her voice was very still and quiet as she whispered, "Please."

Connor dragged in a breath. "How could I say no to that?" he asked, half to himself.

Her laughter was low and enticing. "Of course you can't. It's the magic word. At least that's what we always tell little children."

It wasn't the word, but her that had made it magic. He had Drifter lead him to the end of the table.

"All right, looks like we're ready," Alyssa said, and Connor heard a chorus of children and shuffling shoes enter the room.

"Hey, Connor," Bud called. "You must have heard it was spaghetti night."

It still sounded odd to hear the children use his first name, but Connor had decided to follow Alyssa's lead and go for less formality. He also decided to play along with Bud. "Must have. Tuesday's spaghetti night every week?"

There was a low tittering. "No, it's spaghetti night whenever Alyssa has to cook," Joey whispered loudly at Connor's right elbow. "It's her best dish, but she says she can make other things."

Disbelief laced Joey's voice. "You little scamp," Alyssa teased. "Just for that, I'm cutting spaghetti night from the schedule, and next time I'm making my favorite spinach surprise."

"No, Joey was kidding. We love spaghetti. Spaghetti every night would be just fine," Kanika said with a groan.

"That must be some great spaghetti," Connor mused aloud.

Alyssa swatted him on the arm. The contact was so slight he barely felt it, so quick it was over before it started, but his world still moved. He turned to her immediately.

"I'm so sorry," she said. "Whatever was I thinking?"

"Probably that I'd insulted your cooking," he said, beginning to smile.

"Well then, I'll just have to show you that it's perfectly adequate. The children are well fed. Come on, Joey, Bud, come help me bring in the food. Letice, get the napkins. David, make sure all the glasses are filled. The rest of you put on your best manners. You'll be cleanup crew after dinner."

A groan went down the table.

Alyssa laughed. "Everyone who eats works. Except for Connor tonight. Because he's our guest. Next time he works, too."

"She's a slave driver, isn't she?" he asked.

Letice giggled. "But she works, too, so we don't mind."

Which was a very good point, Connor thought. He hadn't hired her to cook and clean, yet clearly she was willing and able to do so when it seemed necessary.

"Do I pay you enough?" he asked when she returned.

"You pay me enough."

"Should I hire more people so you don't have to do this?"

"No, we like being alone as a family now and then.

Too many people make our lives here together less personal.''

And she sat down beside him. Her rightful place, if she wasn't at the head of the table, would have been opposite him at the long dining table.

For one delicious second, he thought she wanted to be near him. All wrong, of course. It was not a thought he should dwell on, especially since he had a terrible feeling that he knew the real reason she had stayed by his side.

When the meal began and she leaned over and quietly said, ''Spaghetti at eight o'clock and an Italian vegetable casserole at two o'clock. Bread is being passed, the butter is directly north at twelve o'clock, salt and pepper are located at ten o'clock. And yes, I made the casserole, but most of the kids won't touch it, because it has zucchini in it.'' All of this was said very matter of factly, her last comment teasing, as if she'd just been discussing the weather and not helping a full-grown man to find his food.

A part of him hated that she'd had to do that. Alyssa had, no doubt, dated tons of men, none of whom she had had to lead to the butter dish. And while this business of being given directions had always been a part of his life, he rarely needed such assistance these days. He rarely socialized, and he and his housekeeper had a system at home that served him well.

Here, he was a novelty. He didn't want to embarrass himself in front of the children or scare them. But if he were a whole man, Alyssa wouldn't be forced to treat him like a child. Still, she had done it gracefully and without calling attention to him.

"Thank you."

"Oh, you like my spaghetti, do you? See, I told you I was a great cook."

She was bluffing. She knew what he meant, and she'd chosen to ignore it.

What a woman, he thought, twirling some spaghetti onto his fork. "The best I've ever eaten," he said after he'd taken a bite.

Letice snickered.

"Letice," Alyssa drawled. "Are you calling Mr. Quinn a liar? Have you already forgotten that spinach surprise?"

"Oh no, I love this," and it was evident that Letice had a mouthful of food.

"Letice, shame on you," Alyssa teased. "Swallow first, then tell your fibs."

"Shame on you, Alyssa, for accusing her of fibbing," Connor drawled. "This is excellent spaghetti."

"And it doesn't have no meat in it," Bud pointed out, "because Alyssa is a vegetarian and she doesn't like anything unnatural. Nothing that's genet—genet—"

"Genetically altered," Alyssa supplied. "Absolutely, Bud. This is one healthy meal I've made for you with my own two hands. Nothing unnatural about it."

At the world *unnatural,* Connor felt his food stick in his throat. It was a word that had always alarmed him. He'd been called that before, and by a woman, too. There were things about him that just weren't like other men, and Alyssa was a purist. He tried to take a breath and failed, reached for his water and felt his hand push too hard as the crystal toppled and water sloshed every-where.

It was only with great effort that he stopped himself from swearing. A humiliation he'd almost forgotten washed over him as a sudden silence flooded the room and he reached for the glass to right it.

"Damn." It was Joey's voice and it was followed by a crash. "Oh, damn it, I knocked over the saltshaker."

Alyssa tried to look away from Connor's face. It was so very clear that he'd lived this kind of humbling ex-perience before. He was such a strong, sure man, such an intelligent man, a man who clearly valued his con-trol, and here…

"Joey, did you say the *d* word?" she asked with a start, turning suddenly and accidentally sweeping her fork off the table. It hit the oak flooring with a clatter. "Oh, d—"

"Alyssa, you knocked your fork off the table, and uh-oh, you almost said the *d* word, too, didn't you?" Joey asked.

And suddenly Alyssa was under the table, scrounging for her fork. And then Connor was on his knees beside her, crowding close. "Did you do that on purpose?" he asked. "I know Joey did."

She stopped what she was doing and looked up at him. His shoulders were so broad and his eyes such a haunting blue, and suddenly she felt small and soft and feminine in a way she'd never felt feminine before. She wanted to say yes. "No, I wasn't thinking as fast as Joey was. Isn't he clever? Just seven and so fast to jump in there. I do have to do something about that language, though."

"Hmmm, after you nearly said the *d* word yourself?"

And suddenly she was chuckling. "I did, didn't I? Oops. You'll probably want to fire me now. I'm sure I didn't list swearing on my résumé."

"Probably because you're not very good at it. Joey at least got the word out."

"What are you two doin' down there?" Bud asked, leaning over the table upside down.

"I'm teaching Alyssa not to swear," Connor said.

"Well, she didn't really say it," David said. "I'm not sure she even knows how to really let loose with any good swears."

"Let's keep it that way, shall we, David. Don't teach her any if you can help it. I'd like her to stay innocent."

"Yes, sir. I'll make sure the others watch their mouths around Alyssa, too. But it sure would be fun to see her try to do it once. I bet she couldn't even do it."

"I most certainly could. I'll have you know that I could say the *d* word if I really wanted to."

And suddenly Connor was chuckling and all the kids were, too.

"Oh, I can't, can I?" Alyssa said, with some chagrin, although she immediately joined in the laughter.

"It's all right, we like you this way," he said, and he took her hand. Slowly. Deliberately.

She felt it immediately, that thrum in her blood, the feeling that something other than skin and bone joined her to this man. When he touched her, her skin felt more sensitive, she was aware of her body and the very fiber of her being in a way she'd never known before. And this was just a light touch of his hand to hers. What if he touched her more, touched her elsewhere? What if he mated his body to hers, slipped into her depths and wrapped all of him around all of her, warm and naked and touching everywhere?

Her breath stopped dead in her chest, her mind whirled with sensations.

Carefully she pulled her fingers away. "You can't read minds, can you? When you touch me this way, you can't see my thoughts, can you?" She barely whispered the words.

"No." His voice came out quiet but harsh. "But what I can see is too much. I shouldn't do this. Not ever."

"All right, then, we won't," she whispered. "We'll just finish dinner."

But as she took her place at the table again, she knew that dinner was already over, and the night lay ahead.

Hours later she lay in bed, thinking about Connor down the hall. She'd given him a room as far from hers as possible, but still she was absolutely aware of him. He was probably sleeping.

Why not? He'd touched many women in his life, and had had this effect on all of them, she was sure. In other circumstances, with other women, he would not forbid himself to do more. She was the exception, the one he wanted to stay away from, the one he didn't want to affect.

Too late, she thought, cradling her hand to her chest. He had made her want, and now he was going to be like chocolate candy used to be when she'd been a model—something she couldn't have but craved constantly.

* * *

It was still snowing, Connor thought, when he awakened the next morning. Not that he could hear the snow. He couldn't hear anything outside, no plows, no cars on the nearby highway, nothing. Which meant that it had either stopped snowing and the snow was very deep, or the flakes were still falling.

"Hell," he muttered, having no compunction whatsoever about using the *h* word. He had awakened many times last night, and each time he did, he had been in the middle of a heated dream. Himself. Alyssa. Here in this bed. And this time he'd touched her, willingly, deliberately. She'd surged against his hand wantonly. He'd slid his palms up her thighs, over her hips. He'd tasted her lips and her breasts, touched his mouth to her belly and then lower. He'd licked inside of her.

A double shot of pure frustration flooded his body, and he sat up in bed. It was time for an icy shower, because for sure he was still stuck here, and there was no way he could let the woman know just how much he craved her.

"More than coffee," he said as a knock sounded and he called out for the visitor to come in.

"What's more than coffee?" The door swung wide and Alyssa's silky voice greeted him.

"What it's going to take to get me back out on the roads," he ad-libbed. "I take it the snow is pretty deep."

"Yes, you're definitely stuck here with us. The children are all having breakfast. Want some?"

He wanted her, but food would have to do.

"Give me a minute," he said with a nod, moving to throw back the covers.

"Just give me a second to scoot." Her voice was somewhat breathless. He almost wanted to chuckle. She'd thought he was going to parade around in front of her buck naked.

"Not a chance, sweetheart," he whispered to the now-closed door as he climbed out of the bed. "Because if I did, you'd see just how much you affect me."

By the time he made it downstairs, breakfast was almost over, and some of the children were nervously pacing.

"It's like being lost in a snow cave," Wendy whispered. "Kind of eerie."

"Sweet," Bud said.

"Do you think anyone knows we're here?" one of the younger girls whispered.

"Of course, dummy, we were here yesterday. Everybody knows this is the place where the homeless kids live." Bud's voice reflected the sneer that was no doubt on his face.

"What could we do to make this more of a home?" Connor asked suddenly, because while he had loved Jane, and she had tried to make this a loving place, it hadn't really been a home for him, either.

"Nothing, I guess. Gotta have parents for it to be a home."

"It's my home," Joey said shrilly. "I'm not never going to go with new parents again."

"Joey, you and Bud and all of you know that we love you, don't you?" Alyssa asked suddenly. "Just like parents would."

She was right behind him now. He could feel her, and she was wanting him to agree with her that the two of them were like parents. He couldn't. She'd lived this life, too. She knew as well as he did that being loved by an employee or even a benefactor wasn't the same as two people seeking a child out and taking that child home to stay forever. And this conversation was starting because the snow was heavy and powerful and causing a bit of claustrophobia, which always brought out the worst in people.

He felt claustrophobic, Connor thought. Trapped here like a caged beast, he felt too close to Alyssa, too close to his own doubts and desires and limitations.

"Snow like this, it's just too good to waste," he said. "I'm going out. Anyone with me?"

"Connor, some of the kids are still in their pajamas."

He laughed. "Well then, they'd better get changed fast. Snow like this doesn't come all that often. It would be a waste to miss the chance to play in it."

Suddenly the room filled with shrieking and laughter as everyone rushed upstairs to change clothes and find coats and hats and boots and gloves.

He was alone. Almost.

"I'll bet you're pretty proud of yourself, changing the subject like that." Alyssa's voice was right at his ear. Her breath tickled.

Swiftly he turned, cupped her jaw and brushed her lips with his. Just once, just enough to send a bolt of pure, hot agonizing need zipping through his bloodstream.

And then he let her go and moved away.

"I'm very proud of myself," he agreed. "For not doing that sooner. I've been wanting to for days."

She didn't answer.

"Alyssa?"

"Oh my," she said, as if no man had ever kissed her before.

"I should probably apologize, but I don't intend to," he said. "Do you want me to?"

Silence and then she was close again. "No. No. I still don't think we should touch again, but I'm not a fool. I won't deny that I'm attracted, even if I don't want to be."

That got his attention. So she didn't like this heat that ran between them any more than he did.

And she was attracted. It probably would have been best if he hadn't known that. He was obsessing about her enough as it was.

"They adore you, you know. They want to be like you," Alyssa said.

"Not possible. They'll be better than me. They'll be normal. They'll have wives, children."

She stayed close, but she didn't answer, not for a long while. Then finally she cleared her throat. "Don't tell them that, will you? That you don't want kids?"

She was wrong. It wasn't that he didn't want, but that he wouldn't allow himself to sire another aberration. And he wasn't talking about his blindness.

"Connor?" She was worried.

"They'll never hear it from me," he agreed. "Come on, get your coat. I need to cool down. Your lips are very hot, Ms. Fielding."

He was pretty sure that was sputtering he heard, and so he couldn't help his smile. "And by the way, I've noticed a few other things about you. You have a tendency to fidget, to fuss with your clothing and wrist-watch when you're nervous.''

"How embarrassing to be caught. Why do you mention it? Have I offended you in some way?''

"Not at all. I just… Well, I've noticed that you do it most often when you're worried, when you care too much about something. I once implied that you were a bit shallow. Perhaps I was wrong.''

"How magnanimous of you to suggest that you might have a flaw.''

"I have many. As you know.''

"No, I—''

He held up one hand. "We've already established that you're not very good at lying. I just wanted to apologize.''

"Thank you.'' Her voice was very prim. Worried. "Connor?''

"What?''

"Who told you you were flawed?''

He couldn't answer at first. He wasn't going to tell her. "No one.'' Which was a lie and yet the truth. He'd known from the beginning that he was "unnatural.'' If later in life a woman or two had agreed with him, well, they hadn't told him anything he hadn't already known. And Alyssa didn't know the half of it. She worked with handicapped children and she did so with grace and tact and yes, love. But this was a job. She wasn't linked for life to these children, not the way his fiancée had nearly been linked to him.

"You'd better go get warm clothes. The kids are beating us to all the snow.''

"You'll tell me someday, won't you?''

"Tell you what?" he asked.

He thought he heard her sigh, but she left the room. He heard her footsteps on the stairs as she went to get her things.

Eight

Alyssa smiled as she stepped out into the glistening white world and watched Connor carefully rolling snow into a huge ball with two little girls at his side. He had taken Drifter's harness off, and the dog was prancing in the snow like a puppy.

"All right, the rest of you take it from here," he said as he lifted the big heavy snowball onto one that was already formed. "I hope those of you who are in charge of making the head are almost done and that you didn't forget the eyes, nose and mouth."

"I have them right here," Letice said from her place on what Alyssa could only describe as a snow chair, something that looked like a colorful wheelchair with runners rather than wheels.

She must have seen something in Alyssa's expression, because she laughed. "Connor made it for me," she said. "Isn't it cool? It's got snow brakes and everything. Here, guys, two black gumdrops, some red jelly beans for a mouth and a peanut shell for a nose. Now all we need are some arms and a hat and scarf."

Everyone watched as one of the boys came out with the needed items and finished up the snowman.

"He's a little lopsided," Joey said.

"*We're* a little lopsided," Bud said. "All of us have

something a little off, which is cool, just like Alyssa says. Nobody wants to be the same old same old. Right, Alyssa?''

''You said it, Bud.''

''But Alyssa's perfect,'' Letice said wistfully.

Uh-oh. Alyssa opened her mouth. She was very imperfect. Inside she had always been all wrong to many people all of her life. Connor hadn't been the first to doubt her, but she wouldn't bring that up. The kids didn't need or want to hear that their benefactor and their director weren't in harmony.

''Me, perfect? Am not,'' she said. ''I had really bad teeth when I was young.''

''Bad teeth?'' Connor asked in disbelief. She was pretty sure that he didn't doubt her words, but was simply amazed that she could come up with something so lame.

''Yes, and I was really unattractive. One boy called me rat face.''

''Cool,'' Bud said.

''Bud,'' Connor admonished.

''What'd you do?'' David asked.

''Well, I'd like to say that I hit him, but I really just cried. And I had a scar on my forehead from where I fell on some glass.'' She lifted her bangs.

''I don't see it,'' Wendy said.

''Yes, well, I guess it's mostly faded, but it used to be really red and scary looking.

''And another thing,'' she began, but just then a huge snowball hit her square in the chest. She stopped talking, her mouth hanging open. Everyone turned.

Connor was grinning, dusting off the snow on his hands.

"Why did you do that?" she asked. She wanted to ask how he did it, but she'd learned by now that Connor was very tuned in to sounds, and she'd been talking enough to make an easy target.

"I did that because you were getting perilously close to making up some stuff just to make us all feel good. Which we would forgive you for, except that we know you hate to lie. I was just saving you."

"By throwing something at me?"

"It was a snowball, Alyssa," he reasoned. "This is snow. It's for playing in. Sometimes it's for throwing. Because no matter what you looked like as a child— and I'm not sure I believe you were unattractive—we know you're pretty much perfect to look at now."

"How do you know?"

She shouldn't have asked. Was it insulting to ask?

"Have I told you how much I love the fact that you don't tiptoe around my blindness? I *know* you're attractive because you were a model, but also because people have sung praises about your beauty to me. I know because I made it my business to know."

"And now you've made it your business to physically attack me?" Okay, she couldn't help a little verbal battling with him. It was so invigorating. And he was good at it. It was fun.

"If that's what you want to call a good snowball fight. Come on, hit me back."

"I...I can't."

Now he was frowning, angry. "Because I'm blind."

"No, because I don't know how. My parents were

much older than most parents are when they had me. They were not very much fun, and they didn't believe girls should have snowball fights. Then at the orphanage, I pretty much kept to myself. I never learned.''

"So you're pretty much defenseless, then?'' He had a speculative smile on his face.

"You're going to take advantage of that?''

"Oh, absolutely, my dear.'' And he bent to make another snowball. "But I'm betting you have enough champions here to protect you. Joey, Bud?''

"You want us to fight him off, Alyssa?'' Bud asked.

Connor had almost finished his snowball. She loved that he was doing this, but she hadn't been lying. She was going to make a snowball, but she had no faith in her abilities.

"Yes, by all means, get him,'' she said.

And both boys began to pack snow and fire snowballs at Connor. He dodged and ducked with amazing agility but he couldn't dodge them all. "Come on, girls, help me fend them off,'' he said, and soon it was Connor and all the girls against Alyssa and all the boys.

Alyssa bent and tentatively formed a snowball. She fired it at Connor. It fell apart long before it reached him.

"Oh, Alyssa, you were right. You're not perfect. You stink at snowballs, and you throw like a girl,'' Bud whined. "Here, let me show you.'' And he attempted to show her how to pack the snow.

She tried again. It stuck together slightly better, but it hit a tree a good twelve feet away from Connor.

"You just hide here,'' Joey directed, pointing to a bush. "We'll handle the ammo.''

"I am not going to hide while you protect me."

She tried again. She missed big-time.

By now everyone was beginning to laugh and the battle was starting to wane as everyone watched Alyssa repeatedly try to hit a mark.

"You don't even have to dodge, Connor," David groaned. "She's terrible with snow."

"With snowballs," she corrected him. "I can do some things."

"Like what. Show us." Connor was smiling at her. Had a man ever had a sexier smile?

"Well...I could have helped with the snowman, but it's already done. And I can do one other thing, because in spite of my parents' restrictions, I used to slip out and make angels in the snow. It was just too tempting." And she dropped to the ground and began to demonstrate.

"What's she doing?" Kanika asked.

"She's acting nutty," Bud said, "but cool. You know, making angels, swishing her arms and legs in the snow."

"I could swish my arms," Letice said wistfully, and two of the bigger boys helped her out of her chair so that she could enjoy this new experience in the snow. Soon everyone had joined in except Connor.

"Alyssa looks like a real angel," Wendy said.

Which gave Alyssa pause. Her looks had been a sticking point with Connor from the start, and he was still standing in the circle of snow-encrusted children, looking big and awkward and uncomfortable.

She knew that he was self-conscious about certain things that might be considered less than manly. Because of his blindness. Like when he spilled the water or when she'd told him where his food was. She could tell it in the set of his jaw. Apparently making snowballs and snowmen was manly enough, but making snow angels was silly or girlish or just awkward.

She climbed up, walking on her knees to where he stood and gazed up at him. "Please," she said, reaching up to take his hand even though she knew that every time they touched she put herself at risk of succumbing to desire and revealing too much of herself. "I let you try to teach me to throw a snowball, even though I knew I would be hopeless."

He slowly sank to his knees beside her. He leaned closer. "You're a good sport, not hopeless at all, beautiful really. You just need practice." And she knew that by beautiful he didn't mean her face. That touched her, more than anything he'd said to her before.

She pulled his hand to her cheek and pressed gently against it.

He made a move forward. For a moment, they were close. He leaned toward her slightly. She swallowed, wondering if he would kiss her here in front of the children, wondering if she should let him.

"Hey, I don't know what you two are doing, but you still haven't made an angel, Connor," Bud called. "I made one," he pointed out.

"You're a fast one," Connor agreed, and he shrugged and lay back, sliding his arms and legs awkwardly to make an angel.

"Do I look like a fool?" he asked.

"You look like a very big man making a very sloppy but nice angel," Alyssa said.

"Let's make a circle of angels," Letice said. And suddenly Alyssa and Connor were separated by two little girls who were eager to hold someone's hands. One of them, Petra, fell back and latched on to Connor.

"You got to do it smooth, Connor," she said, and together, he and the little girls on either side of them joined hands with all the others. Like skydivers joined in an airy ballet, they made a giant circle of angels.

"We're cool together, aren't we?" Petra asked Connor.

"In more ways than one," he said. And everyone laughed.

"You *are* very cool, Mr. Quinn," Alyssa said with a tinkling laugh, and he wished they were alone so he could tangle his hands with hers, his lips with hers and ask her just what she meant.

"And wet," he agreed.

"Maybe we should all go inside to dry off and have hot chocolate," Alyssa suggested.

A cheer went up, and the kids scampered off to do just that. Soon it was just herself and Connor lying there.

"I can't believe you talked me into this," he said. "It's undignified. I have snow down my shirt."

She chuckled. Immediately he reached out, lifted her and placed her on top of him so that they were lying face-to-face.

For a moment she thought he was going to kiss her. For another moment she was almost sure that *he* thought he was going to kiss her, too. His lips were almost touching hers. Their breath mingled.

Then Connor reached out, and she shrieked as something icy slid down her spine. He smiled.

''You're very cool, too, Ms. Fielding,'' he whispered, his voice rough. With one swift move, he rolled with her, rose to his feet and helped her up.

But as Alyssa stumbled with him into the house, she could have told him that he was wrong. In spite of the snow chilling her skin, every time Connor got close, she grew unbearably hot and lost her ability to reason.

Not a good situation. She needed some fast damage control. Maybe she should just sneak back out in the snow and stay there for a while.

At the very least, she should stop socializing with her boss.

He had belonged today, Connor thought, lying in bed in the night, in a way he had never belonged anywhere before. It was a good feeling, and a frightening one. Best not to get used to it. Definitely best not to get used to the urge to seek Alyssa out and touch her. Even if she stayed, she wouldn't stay forever. From what he'd read on her résumé, it was clear that she was on a fast-track career path. This was just the next step. One day she'd want to move higher. And he was never moving far away from the Haven. It was his tether. It was where he fit.

And besides, she wanted a husband and children. Her own children, he was sure. She would want to go through pregnancy and bear them. He could see that now. But he could never have children. There was too big a chance he might pass on all the horrible things that made him different from the world. He was not normal, and no child should have to live through that. Not again.

But, oh, he wanted to touch her. Inside and out. He wanted his hands on her and he wanted to roll with her on a soft bed with her body tight around his.

What he wanted and what he would allow himself were two different things. He just wished he could stop thinking about her and go back to sleep.

Couldn't be done.

Which was why he heard the dying whir of the heating system. And the muffled cry coming from one of the children's rooms.

"My night-light. It's gone out! It's dark!"

Oh hell, the power had gone out. He knew from past experience that old buildings were large and dark and scary for some of the kids when there were no night-lights. This far away from the lights of the city, the dark would be intense.

Not that darkness and light existed for him, not in the way sighted people saw them. But for most of these kids…

Connor threw off the covers, grabbed a bathrobe and made his way down the hall.

"Petra, it's all right," Alyssa was saying.

"You have other candles?" he asked, moving beside her.

"Yes, a few, but I don't want to risk giving them to the children and starting a fire. We have flashlights, but they cast a rather eerie glow. Some of the little ones are frightened."

He suspected all of the little ones were surrounding them right now. "Ah, that's a shame, then, loves. Darkness can be soothing,'' he said to the children. ''I rather like it myself, but then I don't know light in the way you do.''

''You don't see sunshine, do you?'' Letice asked. She already knew the answer, he was sure. No doubt she'd asked Kanika the same question. Count on Letice to join in making small talk and helping the little ones calm down.

''I feel the warmth. I smell the flowers that the sunshine helps grow.''

''Can you smell the dark?'' Alyssa asked, and suddenly everyone was silent. This was a new question.

''I can smell your candle,'' he said. ''What flavor?''

Someone giggled. ''Flavor,'' a little one said.

''I know I'm supposed to say scent,'' he admitted, ''but don't they come in a bunch of things that sound like flavors now? Vanilla and cinnamon and pumpkin. What flavor does Alyssa have?''

''Lemon,'' Kanika said. ''Smells like lemon.''

''Umm, lemon, you're right,'' Alyssa agreed. ''Let's sit down.''

''Here?'' someone asked. ''On the floor?''

''Why not? It's nice being together like this,'' Connor said and he sat down. The rustling of human bodies and night clothes sounded as everyone sat down.

''What's lemon remind you of?'' he asked. He planned to keep them talking, and soon they would be tired.

''Summer.''

''Lemonade.''

''Picnics.''

The comments and questions and conversation continued for another fifteen, maybe twenty minutes.

Suddenly someone yawned.

"Sorry, I'm tired, and dark as it is, we should be able to sleep better tonight rather than worse," one of the older boys said, and some of the kids wandered back to bed.

But Connor could feel Petra shivering beside him as she contemplated going back to her dark room. "Not ready yet?" he asked, and he felt her shake her head. She must really be scared, because all of the kids had been taught early on to say their answers for the benefit of those who couldn't see.

"All right, we'll tell a story, Alyssa and me," and he began to recite the story of "The Snowy Day."

"How do you know I know that?" Alyssa asked.

He smiled. "I heard you say that it *used* to be your favorite. I think you said it during a moment of stress when you were under attack and being pounded by snowballs."

She laughed, a sound like crystal snowflakes blowing in the wind. "I believe I muttered that under my breath, but oh yes, I remember now. You have ears like a creature of the night."

"I *am* a creature of the night."

"I don't think so. After all, you're the one providing the light here tonight. Symbolically speaking."

But he didn't want to do anything symbolically with her. That was too much like fantasizing, too much like those impassioned dreams that kept him from sleep. So he talked, he told the story, and gradually little heads drooped.

When Alyssa began her part, he started carrying the children back to their beds. No candles necessary. He knew the way, and light, he reminded himself again, was not a part of his life.

Remember that, he told himself.

But when he returned, when they'd told the last bit of story and taken the last child to bed, all that was left was himself and Alyssa. In a sleeping house surrounded by snow and stillness.

He could have warned her not to talk to him, warned her not to draw near to him. The night and the warmth of her body in the chilled building combined to chisel away at his defenses.

"Thank you," she said quietly as they moved down the hallway. And she touched him, softly, lightly, just on his arm.

He came apart inside and lost every argument that told him to step away. Reaching down, he took her hand. He kissed her fingertips and eased his lips to her palm. Then he tugged on her hand and drew her to him.

"Don't thank me. They were frightened. Did you think I would realize that and not do anything to ease their fears?"

"I knew that you would," she whispered. "My first thought when I heard Petra crying was that if you were awake, you would come and you would make her understand about the darkness."

"You don't know what true darkness is," he whispered. "I don't want you to know."

"You're not talking about your sight."

He wasn't, but the truth was that he didn't want to talk at all. He didn't want her to learn any more of him than he'd already revealed. All that he wanted was her. Now.

Connor pulled her close. His lips covered hers, and his mind went crazy with sudden need.

She bumped against him as she opened her mouth and let him inside. Her hands found his shoulders and curved around his neck.

"Kiss me again," she said when he drew back.

"You're sure? We've agreed that we can't get involved," he said. "I don't want to lie to you."

"You're not. We're not meant to be. Except for tonight. We're cut off from everything, and we can be cut off from who we are."

Together they moved to his room, far away from the others. "Teach me to feel the way you feel," she said.

"Can't be done."

"Because you're special."

"I'm not special. I'm different."

"Yes, you're different." And she didn't make it sound like a disease. Because this night was set aside, a few hours separate from the rest of time, he reasoned.

"Is it really true what you said before?" she asked. "That when you touch me you can see my...my outline?" He felt her turn her face from him and tucked a finger beneath her chin, easing her back.

"Your outline is exquisite," he told her, and he raked his palms down her sides, cupping her breasts, spanning her waist, measuring her hips and tracing the long, slim muscles of her legs.

She arched and rose up, kissing him, framing his jaw with delicate hands. "Yours is impressive. I'm closing my eyes, Connor. I know it won't be the same, but I

want to experience you like you're experiencing me."
And without warning she fluttered slender, questing fingers over his chest, down his belly, her hands dipping lower.

"Not yet," he said on a groan. "Not nearly yet." He took her lips, eased her back onto the bed, swiftly unbuttoning her pajama top and stealing it from her as she fell back.

"Exquisite," he repeated, as his knuckles found her bare skin and raked her nipples.

She gasped and he swallowed the sound. He swept what was left of her clothing away, baring her to his touch.

"Now you," she whispered, and she attempted to remove his clothing. "Where did you get this robe?" she asked, struggling with the tight knot.

"Mrs. Morrissey's late husband, gone ten years," he said against her mouth as her awkward fingers nearly drove him mad. "I didn't want to shock anyone."

She smiled against his chest as she made another attempt.

"You can look," he told her, brushing his fingertips over her closed eyelids.

"That would be cheating."

"If you touch me like that one more time, I'm going to expire and then it will be murder. Touch me, Alyssa. Look at me. If I could see you, I would, even if it *was* cheating."

She nodded against his skin. "You see more without sight than I see with my eyes open anyway." She must have opened her eyes, because her movements suddenly became surer. His robe opened, he shrugged out of it, and he felt her shudder as she leaned into him, his arousal up against her belly.

"You're amazingly handsome," she told him, her voice a bit too quiet. "And big."

Her words made him even bigger. He didn't want it. She sounded frightened, but he couldn't help his reaction.

"I won't hurt you," he promised. "Tell me now if you've changed your mind, and we'll go back to bed. Alone." He ground the words out, determined to do just that if she asked him to.

She sucked in a breath. "You think that I could sleep, now that I've seen you and touched you? Touch me, Connor. In every way."

He couldn't suppress the moan that tore from his lips. But he accepted her invitation to feast. He kissed her temple, her eyelids, her nose. He took her lips and drank from her, sliding his tongue over the seam of her lips, then slipping inside to taste all that she was.

Her fingers found him, dancing lightly over his chest, then circling around to clutch at his buttocks as he swirled his tongue around her distended nipple and she arched into him.

Sensations bombarded him. He needed her now, but he'd promised he wouldn't hurt her, and she needed to be made ready.

"Connor, please." She whispered the urgent words.

Sweat beaded his brow. "Not yet. You're not there yet."

Her head swung back and forth. "I'm there. I'm so…"

He reached down between them and found her

hot and slick as he flicked his thumb across her swollen bud.

"There." The word slipped out on a soft wail as she stiffened and arched, losing coordination as the sensations took her.

"Connor," she whispered, and he slipped deep inside her. He braced himself for what he knew was to come, but what happened next was so much more than he was prepared for. Her essence surrounded him, cupped him. She was over and around him and inside him. She held him in all ways; she gave him pleasure too intense to handle.

He fought it, wanting her with him. He wanted to be smooth, but instead he bucked against her. He wanted to hang on, but he couldn't. His body slick with sweat, he braced himself above her and hoped he could bring her one more pleasure. With what little sanity he had left, he touched her again, and she mewled and surged around him.

The world inside his mind released the flood gates of intense pleasure. He cried out as he lost the battle and gave in to sensation. Collapsing, he rolled with Alyssa and dropped into oblivion.

Hours later, somewhere in the night, he reached for her again and she came willingly, both of them sliding into each other's bodies to slowly sate themselves.

Afterward, she yawned and stroked one finger down his cheek. "There will never be another tonight," she said.

"No," he agreed as he kissed her. It would be too risky. He'd used protection, but no protection was one hundred percent effective, and he didn't want to take the chance of getting her pregnant. Never any children. Making love to Alyssa had been indescribably wonderful, but unwise.

So when the morning came, and he discovered she was already out of bed, he told himself he should be glad.

The sound of snowplows filled the air.

It was time to go home.

He was ready, he insisted, as he dressed and went downstairs to a still-quiet house. Of course he was. He heard the sound of a car making its way up the drive. No doubt it was Jerry, here to fetch him and take him back to reality.

"I wonder who that is," he heard her say. "Who would come this early, in that nice a car, in this mess and so soon after the snowplows have passed through?"

Not Jerry. "An overeager salesman?" he suggested.

"Could be. It's a man. He's getting out of the car now, and he looks like he means business."

Her skirt brushed against him as she moved past. "I guess I'd better go see."

"If it's a stranger, I guess I'd better go with you."

"I've been dealing with strangers for weeks."

He remembered the reporters. She'd fended them off alone. "I know. You're a capable woman. I have faith in your ability to send him packing, but I'm hoping you'll grant me the chance to play the big macho role. I'd like the opportunity to send this one away for you."

She laughed. "My hero." For a second she leaned close, and he thought she was going to touch him, kiss him.

But no, that had been last night. This was the morning, and this morning she didn't touch. She let him pass.

Nine

Alyssa was right behind Connor when he opened the door. The man on the doorstep was equal in height to Connor, with black hair and an unreadable expression.

"Connor Quinn?"

"Yes, what can I do for you?" Connor's body blocked the doorway. Alyssa was sure he thought the man might be another reporter.

"Excuse me for barging in so early, but I've been trying to reach you. When telephone service was restored this morning, I reached your housekeeper. She told me you were here."

"And?"

The man was studying Connor's face intently.

"I have information I'm hoping will interest you. Excuse me for being blunt, but this concerns your birth, your family."

Alyssa edged in next to Connor, and she was surprised that he allowed her to share the space. But when she looked up at him, his face was hard and cold. She felt cold, too. She clenched her fingers in the folds of her skirt.

"I don't have a family."

"I'm sure that's what you've been told, but you do have family. More of it than you could know."

"What I have is money. Is that what you're here for?"

"I have money and I don't need more. I'm here because this is all new to me, too. I didn't know about you, but I found out recently. My name is Jake Ingram, and I'm your brother. Not just your brother. We were born on the same day."

Connor's arm at her side was like a rock, cold, hard and unmoving. She reached out and took his hand. He let her. "I think you'd better leave now," he said.

"Not yet." Tension filled the man's low voice. He looked to Alyssa, who was studying him carefully. "Tell him what you see."

"Alyssa?" Connor turned to her. "Go ahead. Do it."

Alyssa closed her eyes, then opened them again. "Take off your glasses, Connor."

For a second she thought he was going to argue, but then he slipped them from his face. Those gorgeous, sightless dark-blue eyes were just as she remembered them, but she'd had to be sure.

"He means," she said faintly, "that he looks a lot like you, Connor. Same height, same hair, although his is slightly darker, and the same eyes. Your eyes looking back at me."

"Seeing you?"

She knew what he meant. "Yes, he's sighted."

For long seconds they all stood there, crowded into the wide doorway. Connor's left hand was a fist, his right gripped hers too tightly, his lips were drawn into a thin line. Finally he uncurled his fingers and loosened his grip, stepping back and drawing her with him.

"Maybe you'd better come inside," he told the man. "May we use your office?" he asked Alyssa.

She almost wanted to smile, remembering how he'd barged into her office two days ago without knocking, but his jaw was taut as a razor, his body stiff and un-yielding, and he slipped his glasses back on.

"Yes, of course," she said quietly. "I'll see to the children. Call if you need anything." She turned to the other man. "I'm Alyssa Fielding, director of Woodland Haven. Would you like coffee, Mr. Ingram?"

"No, thank you. I have everything I need now."

He meant Connor. Clearly he did. Alyssa's mind whirled as she turned away and left the two of them to talk. What would all this mean?

Who knew? Connor didn't look very receptive, but then he'd been caught off guard. He'd spent his whole life being alone. Now he had a brother. That would mean change.

For him.

For the children.

And for her.

Connor motioned to Jake Ingram to take a seat. Then he closed the door and turned toward the man who claimed to be his brother. "I think you have some ex-plaining to do."

"More than you know."

Connor waited. He tried not to decipher his feelings or even to feel at all, although a growing sense of dread was building inside him. He didn't want to think about the fact that when he'd awakened this morning, he'd been reaching for Alyssa, even though he'd known their night had ended. All his life he'd been alone. There was safety in the familiarity of being alone.

"How do you know I'm your brother? Other than what Alyssa said, that we look alike? How did you find me?"

The man on the other side of the desk cleared his throat. "It wasn't easy finding you, believe me. As to how I know I'm your brother, that takes some explaining and some time." He waited.

"I have time," Connor said.

"Good. It's an unusual story. It seems that in the 1960s a scientist, Henry Bloomfield, was experimenting with genetic research. He wanted to create perfect human beings in a controlled environment. Under ideal circumstances, the guesswork of human reproduction would be eliminated. There would be no flaws, no mistakes. A parent could choose the attributes he or she wanted in a child, even enhance those attributes to an amazing degree. In time his work, which was funded by the government in a secret project called Code Proteus, came to fruition. Henry's assistant, Violet, was artificially inseminated with Henry's donated sperm, and three babies, designed to have certain traits, were born."

Conner took an audible breath. His heart began to beat harder, faster.

Jake paused.

"Go on."

"I suppose you can guess that you're one of those babies. So am I, and we have a sister named Gretchen."

Connor struggled for air and rational thought. He felt dizzy, nauseated, but when he felt Jake lean toward him he waved him away. "I thought this Henry Bloomfield was aiming for perfection."

"He was."

Connor took off his glasses again. He raised his head. "I won't bother stating the obvious. What sort of traits was I supposed to have?"

"Mathematical and technological skills."

Connor jerked.

"Not a failure," Jake said slowly. "Your company creates some amazing items."

Connor ignored the compliment. "So how did we become separated and why are you here now?"

He heard the legs of Jake's chair slide slightly and felt him lean into his space over the table again. "Just recently I found lab notes. When you were born, Henry saw evidence that you were blind. He assumed he'd failed, as did his scientist associates. Without telling anyone, Henry sent you to Woodland Haven and set up a trust fund for you. He told Violet that you had died. That was the last anyone associated with the experiment saw of you."

"I knew about the trust fund. It was anonymous. Our father obviously didn't want to be known or to know me." And when he had reached his majority, Connor had turned the remainder of the fund over to the orphanage. "So he dropped me at a convenient location, and the rest of you went on with your lives. I assume you're a success."

"Don't assume anything, brother of mine."

"What does that mean?"

"It means that nothing concerning your life or that of your brothers and sisters is easy or simple. And there's more. A couple of years after you and I and Gretchen were born, three more, Marcus, Faith and Gideon, came along. All have special qualities that have been genetically engineered, just as you do. But that wasn't the end of things. The two other scientists, Agnes Payne and Oliver Grimble, who worked on the project, wanted to take control. They wanted to use the children for their own purposes, but they didn't know all the details of Henry's research. And once he realized that they were desperate and dangerous, Henry took steps to keep them from knowing. The five remaining children grew up, until Gretchen and I were twelve.

"Then, concerned that such useful tools as we were, were going to get away from them, Oliver and Agnes began to do 'experiments' on us, exercises in mind control. They murdered Henry and planned to get Violet to reveal his secrets by using threats to the children as leverage. But they also wanted to be able to use the powers that my brothers and sisters and I had been given for their own purposes, so they drugged Violet and then, using hypnosis, suppressed all of our memories.

"Violet was able to get us away, to steal us away, and she sent us all to safe homes, where we grew up, as unaware of each other's existence as you've been. It's only been in the past few months that we've been brought together."

Connor was reasonably certain that he didn't want to hear the rest of the story, and just as certain that he couldn't bear to remain ignorant.

"How did you find me? *Why* did you find me?"

"Violet was able to get all of her children away except one son, one she thought had been shot and killed. Now, years later, she discovered she was wrong. Oliver and Agnes have been trying to decipher Henry's codes for years, and they've made use of the one son they were able to maintain control over. They call themselves the Coalition, and they've become quite powerful. I'm sure you've read all about the World Bank Heist and Achilles, the mastermind behind it.''

Connor sat up straighter. ''Are you trying to say that this has something to do with us?''

''Everything. When Violet read the news, she knew that Achilles was Gideon, her lost son. I was already looking into the World Bank Heist, so she hunted for me until she found me, and I've hunted for all the rest. Except for you. I didn't know about you.''

''Because I'm not a part of your family, Mr. Ingram.''

''Damn it, you are.'' The sound of papers being pushed from the table sounded as Jake placed his hand on Connor's arm. ''I know that you are.''

''How?''

''Henry's lab notes, scribbled in the margin. He gave you up, but he made sure you were cared for. I searched the homes for children born in 1967, and I found one, born blind, with abilities that might seem like mere genius to the average human being, but they're not simple genius, are they? They're more, beyond the comprehension of other humans. You're different, like me. And like Gretchen and Marcus and Faith and Gideon.''

''How are they different? How are you different?''

''Some say I'm a financial wizard. Gretchen can solve the toughest puzzle. She's a cryptologist. Marcus has extraordinary strength, and Faith is a gifted physician and diagnostician.''

''And Gideon, what can he do?''

''He's gifted in the fields of math and technology.''

''Excuse me?'' Connor's voice felt as if it was coming from a long distance away, faint and hollow.

''He's you,'' Jake said slowly. ''They tried again, and they succeeded. Again.''

Connor felt as if he'd been kicked in the head. With something very hard. He felt pain flash behind his eyes. Dizziness nearly made him bend over, but he forced himself to stay upright. ''They wanted someone perfect this time.''

''I won't apologize for my father. Giving a child up because he doesn't meet expectations, even if you provide for that child, is an unforgivable act. But that wasn't Violet. She didn't know. She grieved for you then and right up until her death.''

''How do you know? You were a baby like me.''

''She mentioned it. She wrote it in her diary.''

But she hadn't known what his father had known, that he was imperfect. Would she have grieved if she had? Anger rose up black and heavy within him. ''So you've come to me out of…what? Guilt? Curiosity?''

''I won't lie. I have more than one motive in coming to you. For years, with my memory suppressed, I didn't even know my family existed. Now that I do, I want all of us back together. I want to know my brothers and sisters, and I would have fought to find them no matter what. But there's more.''

Connor shook his head. ''Explain.''

''As I said, I'm investigating the World Bank Heist.

I need help finding the headquarters of the Coalition. I need someone who can help me find Achilles. Gideon.''

"I'm not a detective.''

"No, you're not. You're better. You're Gideon's brother. You're my triplet. And Gretchen's. But you're also Gideon's genetic twin in many ways. There are things you know about him, things you understand that I don't.''

Jake's words rang in the room, then died away. Connor sat there with the weight of all Jake had said pressing down on him. Doubts bombarded him, and he wanted to reach out. But more than that, he wanted to deny, to run. This was a man investigating the World Bank Heist. He needed someone talented in math and technology, and Connor knew that he was the best. Wouldn't a man like that, like Jake, say anything, make up any lie? And why wouldn't it be possible to fake a few physical characteristics? Hair could be dyed, eye color could be changed with contact lenses.

"You expect me to just accept all this, to take you at your word?''

"I don't have the right to expect anything. I'm merely hoping you'll believe me.''

He didn't want to, but dread ran deep in him, and Connor realized that he'd always known there was something unnatural about him. Now he knew why.

"What if I don't help you?''

Jake let out a deep sigh. "Oliver and Agnes want to do more than grow rich and disrupt the world. They want to run it. They'd like nothing better than to be able to decipher Henry's notes and figure out how to replicate his experiments, produce more people like us.''

''Misfits.''

''Perhaps, but very powerful, nonetheless. If they produce more children of our ilk, they won't have any concerns about ruining the lives of those children, of using them. They agreed with Henry that you were not of value. They tried to steal my life and that of my other brothers and sisters. They did steal Gideon's life, and forced him to turn to evil. Because of them, Violet is gone. We have to stop them. You could help do that.''

''I can't make that decision right now. This requires more careful thought.''

Jake gave a rough laugh. ''The consummate mathematician. Study a situation from all angles. I'll leave you, then, but...''

''What?''

''We don't have much time. They know that we're after them, and they're smart. Moreover, they've got Gideon who's beyond smart. You should know.''

Connor grunted. The legs of Jake's chair scraped across the floor. ''May I say hello to your dog?''

''If he'll let you. This is a...a friend, Drifter.''

''I'll let that pass for now. It's better than enemy. But you should know that I'm determined to bring you into the fold and introduce you to the rest of us.''

Connor stood. ''We'll see.'' But he knew that it wouldn't happen. He'd been alone all his life. It was what helped him to function, and it was too late for family now.

He listened as Jake moved through the house, said goodbye to Alyssa, then left.

She didn't come inside her office. He'd known that she wouldn't. It was for the best. His thoughts wouldn't leave him alone. He'd always known that his blindness separated him from the world in some ways, but the other thing, that had been the real difference. Now he knew why. He wasn't real. He was a product, an invention, not much different from the products he invented.

And his difference scalded him. It separated him from all that he wanted.

And he did want, he realized now. He wanted Alyssa in his bed...and more. She was a beautiful woman who should have a man to appreciate that beauty, not a man who couldn't even see all that she was.

She wanted children.

What kind of children, what kind of aberrations, might a man like himself produce?

None. It wasn't possible. His very DNA had been contaminated. Blindness could be the least of the traits he might pass on.

His heart was like a dark, cold stone. He had to get out of here. He had to go somewhere and think. Or not think.

Yes, it was best not to think at all. He put in a call to Jerry.

"I'm just down the road, boss. Just waiting. I figured you'd be wanting to get home."

"Good. Come now, please."

He sat there for minutes, realizing that he hadn't lost his family. He'd been given away. He had brothers and sisters, all mutations like himself. He wanted to hug the secret to himself, the way he always had.

Please, God, don't let her find out, he thought as he stalked from the room behind Drifter.

He was nearing the door when he heard her and breathed in her scent.

"You're leaving?"

"Yes." He couldn't say more.

"Was that man really your brother, then?"

"I don't know. Probably." He wished his voice didn't sound so angry. It was like a slap, but he couldn't manage to stop. "Look, I've got things to do. Work. I'll call you."

"Of course." Her voice was small and clipped. He realized his last sentence had sounded like something a man said after he'd slept with a woman and wanted to end things with no fuss.

He should stop, turn to her, touch her, hold her, reassure her. At least talk to her.

But his voice and his sanity were trapped inside him somewhere. Or maybe they were lost forever. What was left wasn't of much value to a woman.

He left the building without saying another word.

"He left and he didn't say he was coming back?" Alyssa whispered to herself. "So what? It wouldn't be the first time you've been rejected."

But it would be the first time in years that she'd cared.

She *did* care. Because Connor wasn't just any man. She didn't let just any man into her bed. There had to be friendship, caring, something other than just lust.

"There's not more than lust," she muttered. He'd made it clear that he didn't want anyone like her. He didn't want dreams or marriage or children.

So, touching her, making love with her had been the kind of thing he might do with any woman.

Except he was Connor.

She was betting that he didn't come to a woman's bed lightly. He didn't do anything lightly. And that man, Jake Ingram, the one who looked like Connor, had been in that room with him for a long time. What had he told Connor?

Something bad. Something he hadn't wanted to hear.

Connor wasn't a cruel man, even though he might appear cold to some. He was…

She didn't dare finish that sentence, but the words came to her anyway. Connor was a man she was perilously close to loving.

And who *was* Jake Ingram really? If he was messing with Connor, well…

"Well, I'm just going to be very ticked," she said. Nobody took advantage of her children and no one waltzed in and turned Connor from a man who could touch a woman and make her cry to a man who was grim and cold as January nights.

"So what are you going to do?" she asked herself.

But the obvious answer was a bleak one. Nothing. She could do nothing.

She may have shared Connor's bed, but that didn't mean there was anything between them. He was her employer, she was his employee. There were no promises between them.

When it came down to the truth, there was nothing lasting between them. Connor had made that abundantly clear.

* * *

Connor sat on the floor of his study, a bottle of beer in his hand. Around him stretched a small collection of other bottles. They clattered against each other as he moved.

Drifter lay at his side, ever vigilant.

"I've done nothing but hurt her from the start, boy," he said. "I rejected her as an employee, insulted her professionalism, then I took advantage of her on a dark night when she was susceptible. I used my powers to coax her to my bed," he said, rubbing his hand over his thigh as if to erase that power. "And then I just walked out on her. I'm an ass."

But he was more than an ass. He was...

"I don't know who or what I am. Not really. I'm an aberration, an experiment. And one gone wrong, at that."

Not completely wrong, apparently, but no one knew that. No one knew about his powers except Jake and himself.

Jake. Family. A brother? Was it true?

Connor closed off the emotions that bombarded him. He didn't want emotions or need or family. Being alone was safer, a constant, no risks.

But even if they weren't related, Jake wanted his help to find Gideon. He knew that much to be true. When he'd gotten home, he'd sifted through every on-line news article on the World Bank Heist that he could find. Whoever had committed the crime had been a true genius.

Was Achilles Gideon? Did Gideon even exist? Did he, Connor, have a brother who had powers like his own? And what if he did what Jake had asked him to do? What would happen if he tried to find Gideon?

"Might do it," he said, his speech slightly slurred. "But if I did, that might attract attention to those others. Who were they? Oliver and Agnes. A bad lot. Dangerous. They might want to hit out at me. How would they do that?"

The answer made his breath stop cold. The fog cleared from his mind. If he had an enemy who wanted to hurt him, that enemy would hit him where he could be hurt. Through Alyssa and the kids.

Pain shot through his head. Awareness. Sudden clarity. His body was on fire, his fingers tingled.

"No. That won't happen. I won't think about it." But he knew he would.

Oliver and Agnes were going to try to make more children, genetic aberrations. Nausea clogged his throat at the term, but he didn't back away from it. It was, after all, the bitter truth. And these monsters, these scientists, were going to use those children, control them, hurt them if someone didn't step in and put a stop to things.

If he tried to stop them, he risked Alyssa and Joey and all the rest.

He would never hurt Alyssa. It was why he'd tried so hard to stay away from her, why he would make a greater effort from here on out to keep away from her.

Alyssa. Even thinking her name made him want to howl with need. He'd wanted things before that he couldn't have. Not like this. No use thinking about this. Connor tried to turn from his thoughts, but there was no escape, at least no permanent escape. He didn't believe in losing oneself in alcohol, but then, he didn't believe in a lot of things. He didn't believe in family, but his family or lack of it had always been there, a part of him. Not a good part, either. Now Jake had held out family like a lure. A stupid man would bite. He wasn't stupid, but God help him, he couldn't ignore the man or his words, and that was why he was going quietly insane. He clutched his bottle and drank deeply.

Ten

Agnes Payne hung up the phone and turned to Oliver. "Jake Ingram has been making discreet inquiries at foundling homes. What do you make of that?"

"I don't know. Maybe he's looking for a sidekick or maybe he's looking to adopt a child." His tone didn't indicate that he believed either of those things.

"Or maybe he's looking for something else. Ingram has been single-minded about his quest to find the perpetrators of the World Bank Heist ever since we pulled it off. Not that he's ever going to be ahead of us on this one, but you can believe that if he's talking to foundling homes, there's a reason for it, and the reason has to do with us."

"So what are we going to do?"

"Watch him. Find out whatever it is that he's found out. Figure out what it is about a foundling home that has attracted his attention. And then use that information to our advantage."

"How?"

"In any way we can, my dear. As always, we use it in any way we can."

He had left her like a man who couldn't wait to get away, Alyssa thought two days later. Two days and she hadn't heard a word from Connor. Not a note, not a phone call.

What had taken place in her office with Connor and Jake Ingram? What had happened that had caused Connor to turn from a man who made love that melted her very soul to a man who brushed her aside as he closed the door in her face?

Anger, hot and powerful and frightening, coursed through her. He had thought her a bit of fluff from the minute he met her—even before he met her. He had made snap judgments about what she was like and what she was or, rather, was not capable of.

And now a man shows up at the door, claiming to be his long-lost brother—no, more than a brother, he'd said—and Connor had put on a fresh, cold mask of indifference.

"But he's not indifferent," she whispered. She'd seen chinks in that cold armor of his, flashes of humanity, hints of caring for the welfare of these kids, traces of vulnerability.

What had Jake Ingram said to him? What had he done to him? Had Connor had second thoughts about having opened up to her, or had something gone on in that room with Jake that had sent him back behind his impregnable walls?

"Well, Alyssa, you can spend all this time worrying and speculating or you can call the man and find out."

She picked up the phone and dialed. After many rings, Connor's housekeeper, Mrs. Welsh, answered. "I'm sorry, Mr. Quinn is…unavailable."

Pain sliced through Alyssa. He didn't want to talk to her. Then reason settled in. Connor was a businessman, a busy man. Of course there would be times when he would be unavailable to take calls.

Several hours later she tried again. She left messages, both at his home and at his office. All went unanswered.

Panic began to climb within her. Connor might well be having second thoughts about having gone too far with her, but she knew that he would never neglect the kids, and she was his doorway to the kids. If he wasn't taking calls from her, it was beyond personal. It was bigger than what had taken place in her bedroom. It had something to do with the appearance of his brother, and she had a feeling it was very bad.

What had Jake Ingram done to Connor?

And where *was* Connor? Was he sick? Was he gone?

She tried his home again.

When the housekeeper answered, Alyssa changed her tack. ''Please tell Mr. Quinn that I'm calling as the director of Woodland Haven.'' It was only partially a lie. As the director, she needed to have access to Connor. And even if it was a complete lie, that was just too damn bad.

The housekeeper's voice came back on the line. ''Mr. Quinn is indisposed, but he did say that he respects your ability to handle any crisis with Woodland Haven. You are to have any money or resources necessary to carry out your work.'' Mrs. Welsh was a genius at hiding her reactions, but even so, Alyssa thought she detected a trace of concern in her voice.

''Is he all right?''

''He's…he's unavailable.'' And Mrs. Welsh hung up.

That did it. That catch. Something was drop-dead

wrong. Alyssa wanted to scream, to do and say all the wrong things, to run over to Connor's house, do whatever it took to get inside and confront the man.

Who would no doubt give her an icy cold shoulder and request, politely but firmly, that she get the hell out of his house and his life.

Okay, so confronting Connor while she was still in the dark as to what had happened would get her nowhere. And he'd never let her near enough to find out a thing. Jake was the key.

But how did she find Jake?

Maybe she didn't. Jake had obviously searched high and low to find Connor, so he was, no doubt, a man who kept his finger on the pulse of what was going on. If she left a few crumbs out, maybe he'd find her. And maybe then she could figure out what was going on with Connor.

For the children's sake, she told herself.

Yes, that was true, but she also had other reasons for her unwillingness to let this go. And she didn't want to think about them.

Instead, she picked up the phone and called Connor's house. The housekeeper answered.

"I'm sorry to disturb you again, but this is Alyssa Fielding. I believe a Mr. Jake Ingram may be trying to get in touch with Mr. Quinn. If Mr. Ingram calls, would you mind letting him know that I'm trying to reach him, and that it's very urgent."

The woman hesitated.

"Please," Alyssa said. "It's extremely important."

"All right," the woman said. Alyssa thanked her and

called Connor's office, where she left the same message. Finally, she called Jerry, Connor's driver.

"He hasn't been out in two days. Not that unusual, though," Jerry admitted. "But if I hear from Jake Ingram, I'll let him know you want to talk to him."

There, Alyssa thought, when she hung up. That was all she could do.

For now.

Jake hung up the phone and stared at the receiver. Another frustrating conversation with Tara. She was upset with him because he was so unavailable. Because she didn't know what was going on, he thought. And as his fiancée she probably had a right to know more than she did.

"I should tell her," he said, but he knew that he couldn't do that yet. There was far too much at stake.

That should probably mean something to him.

He didn't want to figure out what it was.

Instead, he picked up the phone to call Connor. He'd given his brother three days. He'd posted an agent to keep watch over Connor's house and make sure that nothing suspicious happened. Nothing had. No one from the Coalition knew, then.

And Connor had had time enough to decide whether he would help.

Time was too important. He couldn't wait any longer.

The phone picked up on the second ring.

"Quinn residence."

"Excuse me, I'm looking for Mr. Quinn. If you could tell him that Jake Ingram is calling, I'd appreciate it."

"I'm sorry, but Mr. Quinn is unavailable."

"I think he'll talk to me."

"I think not. He told me that you might call, and he still said that he wasn't receiving any calls."

"Hell. Tell him—"

"But Ms. Fielding wanted to talk to you. She said it was very important."

Ms. Fielding? The director of the foundling home. Damnation. What did she know? Had Connor spilled sensitive information to her?

"Thanks." He hung up the phone, already reaching for his coat and heading for his car. As he moved, his bodyguard fell in line with him. Jake barely flinched anymore when that happened. Disconcerting and annoying as it was, it was necessary and left him free to tend to important things.

Within a much shorter time than should have been possible had he not been practically standing on the accelerator, Jake pulled up in front of Woodland Haven. He was out of the car and at the front door in a matter of seconds.

Alyssa Fielding must have been waiting and heard his car pull up. Because she turned and looked behind her. "Edwina, I have to go out for just a short while. I'll be at the new grounds if you need me."

She led him away from the home. "The workers are gone for the day. We can talk there without anyone hearing." She moved on, her boots crunching on the snow as she headed for the almost finished building.

"What are we talking about?" He played dumb.

She whirled suddenly and faced him, her eyebrows drawn together in consternation.

"What did you say to Connor the other day?"

He raised one brow. "What do you mean?"

"He's suddenly unavailable to anyone. He loves these kids, but suddenly he won't even come around, he won't even talk to me. Something's wrong. Really, terribly wrong. I think you know what it is. I want you to either tell me what it is or I want you to fix it."

Alyssa retraced her steps until she was standing beside him. She was a tall woman, a fierce woman, Jake noted.

Her fierceness didn't fit her fragile appearance, but it was still real. Mother-bear real. I'm-going-to-make-you-suffer-if-you-don't-come-clean real. The thought made Jake want to smile, but he couldn't. Her words disturbed him too much.

"You mean that no one's seen him?"

She shook her head. "I suppose his housekeeper has. She isn't letting any calls through, though. He hasn't been in to work, and his driver says he hasn't been anywhere."

And maybe he wasn't even at home. Maybe he'd been taken away. Had Oliver and Agnes somehow figured out what was going on and located Connor? Had they gotten through to the housekeeper?

"Damn, how well do you know his housekeeper?"

"Not well, but enough to know she'd lie for Connor. She'd cover for him if she could."

Something in Alyssa's voice stopped Jake from asking her if she would do the same. A concern, a fear, an anger. "It's none of my business, I'm sure," she began, "but I'm making it my business. Connor was raised in this home, he was given away as a baby, he's never known any family at all. And then you come in here and claim to be family and now he's closeted himself away from anyone.''

''I *am* family.''

''I know, but what kind of family? The good kind or the other kind?''

''I don't want him hurt.''

''But what you said touched off something in him. I want to know what it was. Whether you want him hurt or not, something you said damaged him in some way. That's not acceptable.''

''You have a claim on Connor?''

She paused at that. Hot color flooded her face. Ah, so there was something going on there, Jake realized. The lady was more than just the director of this school. Then she shook her head. ''I don't want to see him hurt,'' she said, stubbornly refusing to elaborate.

''And what would you do if I said that I was here to harm him?''

Alyssa drew herself up to her full height. She raised her chin. ''I would do what I could to stop you.''

''Brave lady, but words are easy.''

''Not always. Sometimes they're very difficult.''

The spark of honesty shone from her eyes, and he didn't have to ask any more questions. Not really. He'd already researched everyone intimately connected with Connor. The lady rated. In more ways than one. That warrior queen's look in her eyes touched him in that place where brotherly love was starting to grow. He wondered if Connor knew what he had in this woman. He wondered if Tara would offer to aid him in the same way if the tables were turned.

''All right, then,'' he conceded. ''I'll tell you what I

can. You know him better than I do. Perhaps you know a way in for me."

Confusion filled her eyes. "What do you mean?"

"I am Connor's brother, and though we were separated at birth, I care about his well-being. But I'm also a man investigating a case, and Connor may be able to help me. I've told him what I can of the case. It's not an easy decision for him to make. Helping me, even just being who he is, may put him in danger. He may be in danger already."

The woman's eyes darkened, grew round with fear. For herself, or for Connor, he wondered. "What kind of danger?"

"The people I'm looking for may want to harm Connor or even get rid of him, but most likely they want to use him. Connor has…abilities beyond the range of most of the human race."

"I know." And he could tell from her eyes that she did indeed know.

"You came here to warn him?" she asked.

"Partially. I also came here to find and claim my brother. And—" he studied her carefully "—as I said, I came here to ask him to let me use his powers."

She took a deep, visible breath. "Would that put him in more danger?"

"I'm afraid it will definitely place him in greater jeopardy."

Her eyes darkened as mist clouded them. "How could you do that? He's your brother. He's been deemed unimportant before. How could you make him feel like that again? To tell him that his safety is less important than your case?"

Jake looked to the side. "He's very valuable and not just because of what he's capable of. I care, Alyssa, but I couldn't not ask. The lives and fate of many are at stake. I need Connor."

"To sacrifice himself." She spat the words out.

"I'll protect him as much as I can. I don't want him hurt." Jake barely got the words out, so intense were his feelings.

"If you hurt him, you'll have me to deal with," she said, and she turned and whirled away.

He watched her walk away, then called out. "You're a formidable lady, Ms. Fielding. What are you going to do?"

"I'm going to him."

He digested that information, then nodded slightly. "Tell him…"

"Yes?"

"Tell him I'm sorry for everything, and tell him I hope we'll all be able to get together—all of his brothers and sisters—soon under better circumstances."

She nodded tightly.

"Alyssa?"

"Don't tell anyone. If you haven't already, don't tell anyone about Connor's powers."

She studied him with blue eyes that searched. He knew she suspected his motives, and why not? He was a stranger who had come in and messed up her world and his brother's life.

"It was never my secret to tell anyway. I would never do or say anything that I thought would harm him. I don't think Connor appreciates his gifts or wants anyone to know."

"I understand."

"Do you?"

"More than you know."

She stared at him then, and he believed that she really did know. The woman looked inside a person far too easily. She was far too empathetic for her own good. He wondered if she knew that. He wondered if Connor did.

She worried about Connor being hurt, but he knew—oh yes, he knew all too well—how he and his kind could hurt others. They were different.

And they hid it.

And that hurt.

Connor was at risk, but so was she.

When things settled down, he was going to have to have a talk with his brother about that.

Just as soon as he got his own life in order.

Back in the house Alyssa packed some clothes. Please, God, let him let her in his house. She couldn't even begin to think of what she'd do if he didn't let her inside.

"Edwina, I've called Nola, and she has agreed to be here whenever you're not. I'm sorry to have to leave you so suddenly, but I have a personal emergency I have to tend to. You can reach me at this number." She handed the scrap of paper to the teacher who studied it. It was clear that the woman knew whose number it was, but to her credit, she didn't say a word.

Then Alyssa gathered the children together.

"I'll be back just as soon as I can. And I'll call and drop in every day," she told them. "But if you need anything, anything at all, you let one of the teachers or Mrs. Morrissey know. And if you get scared, you tell them that, too. I'll only be a short distance away.''

"Are you sure you're coming back, Alyssa?" Kanika asked sadly.

"I promise that I am, love."

"If you see Connor, will you tell him that I'm working on a new invention?" Bud asked.

"Absolutely, I will."

"Tell him I'm going to win again at Monopoly the next time," Joey said.

Alyssa hoped there would be a next time. She realized that leaving the children was much harder than she had ever anticipated. She gave each one a hug, then quickly exited the house before the lump in her throat became tears.

Within a half hour she was pounding on Connor's door.

The housekeeper met her.

Alyssa could see that Mrs. Welsh was going to try to give her an excuse.

"Forgive me," Alyssa said softly, and she shoved hard past the woman, heading toward the back of the house.

He was here somewhere. She only hoped he wasn't dead set on getting her out of here.

Connor was much bigger than his housekeeper. If he wanted her gone, she was going to have a fight on her hands.

Eleven

There was a commotion at the door. Connor heard Mrs. Welsh shriek and then there was a thump and a soft "forgive me" that sounded so much like Alyssa that Connor felt a pool of need shoot through him.

"I'm hallucinating, Drifter," he said, touching his dog for sanity's sake. Drifter lifted his head and rubbed against his hand. "She wouldn't come here, would she? Unless there was a problem with the children. With Joey? Hell, what kind of a selfish bastard have I been?"

His last words were muttered just as the door to his room flew open.

"Connor?"

Alyssa's soft voice broke in, and he rose from his chair, shoving one hand back through his hair. "What are you doing here?"

"What are *you* doing to yourself? You look as if you haven't slept in days. You need rest."

He hadn't slept, at least not much. "I'm fine."

"You're not. If you were, you would have spoken to me directly instead of leaving Mrs. Welsh to give me the brush-off."

"I wasn't brushing you off, Alyssa."

"The hell you weren't."

She blew out a breath, an audible sound of disbelief,

and he did his best to try to pull himself together. He stood straighter, counting on the breadth of his shoulders to intimidate. His lips firmed into a hard slit. "I informed you that I trusted you to do your job. If you're here, I can only assume that there's a problem with the school."

"You know what the problem is."

But he wasn't going there, and he certainly wasn't going to drag her down with him. He had to get her out of here.

"The problem seems to be that you've forgotten that you're my employee."

He heard her suck in her breath in a small gasp, then move toward him. "The problem is that you seem to think that giving only works one way. You can give, but you can't take, Connor."

"There's nothing I need to take."

"Well then, that makes one of us." Her voice turned low and smooth and husky. He did his best not to notice, but the battle had already been lost.

"I can't give you what you need," he said.

"Oh, you're so wrong, Mr. Quinn. I know that whatever it was that Jake told you, you think it's your problem alone. But it's not. I can help, and *you* can give me exactly what I need." She walked up to him and wound her arms tightly around his neck. She pressed herself against him.

He could feel her shivering. Her heart was tripping along at triple time, but he didn't think that it was desire causing her reaction. She was nervous, afraid, but for some reason she wanted him to think she needed his touch.

He tried to ignore her soft skin, her delicious scent, her selfless act of trying to distract him away from his troubles. He did his best not to touch her. He wouldn't, except to put her away from him.

Connor reached up behind his neck to disentangle her fingers.

She rose up on her toes and touched her lips to his.

His mind stopped working, his breathing and heartbeat nearly stopped, too. Her lips were soft and sweet and moist, and she tasted of mint and honey.

He needed her.

A low groan tore from his lips, and he slid his arm around her back and trapped her against him. He kissed her.

"Don't do this," he whispered. "You don't know what you're doing."

"I know I don't. I'm operating purely on instinct and need."

"My need," he said.

And she pulled one of his palms against the soft curve of her breast. Her nipple poked against cloth and seared his palm.

"*My* need," she whispered. "Touch me, Connor."

His answer was to brush his lips across hers. She reached up and sank her fingers into his hair.

He plunged his hands into hers and kissed her again. One time. Ten times. He lost count, and it didn't matter, anyway. All that mattered was this moment and her body against his.

At some point he waltzed her backward toward the couch. At another point he slipped open the zipper on the simple sheath she wore. He whisked it away from her, leaving her only in two lacy bits of nothing.

"Take them off," he said.

"You do it. With your teeth."

He couldn't help smiling then. It was the first time he'd felt like smiling since his brother had stepped into his life. "You're the prim and proper woman the board hired to run the school?"

"I never said I was prim and proper. But I am, most of the time."

"And what about the rest of the time?"

"Then I'm not. When I'm with you I'm not. It's the only time."

"Good." He reached down and released the clasp of her bra. With one quick, smooth move, he had removed her barely-there panties. She was naked now, and she was his. For this moment, anyway. Later there would be complications. Barriers.

He intended to let those barriers stand.

But not now.

Now he didn't have the strength to keep fighting his own desires and needs. And what he needed right now was Alyssa's nakedness covered by his body.

He needed that connection, that sense of being one with her, the feeling that he wasn't alone.

Only she could give him that.

She was offering.

He was taking, but he also intended to give to her if he could. He had hurt her by disappearing suddenly and then refusing to take her calls. It had been necessary but cruel.

He just couldn't be cruel to her tonight.

"Come," he said, lifting her and sliding beneath her so that her nude body topped his fully clothed one. "Let me apologize to you." And he kissed the crest of her breast.

Her body jerked, and she let out an astonished moan.

"Let me show you that I'm truly sorry for being such a cold bastard," he continued. He slicked one hand up her arm, lifting her hair from her neck as he pulled her closer and trailed kisses down that slender, sensitive column.

"Let me do more," and he raked his fingertips over her hip, skirting her thigh and resting his palm on her curls, his thumb tangling deep as he caressed her.

She writhed and squirmed against him, her breath coming hard and fast. "No, let me." And her small delicate hands clutched the front of his shirt and pulled hard, popping buttons. She leaned forward and placed her lips on his chest, nibbling her way to one nipple.

His entire body surged and went on alert.

"Lady, you're killing me," he moaned, planting his hands on her hips to lift her from him. Or pull her closer. He was beyond figuring out which.

Too late, anyway. She made quick work of removing his pants, and then they were together, nothing separating them.

In a matter of seconds he would be where he wanted to be. Embedded in her warmth, surrounded by her passage, lost to passion and oblivion and ecstasy.

Capable of making a baby.

Connor gritted his teeth. He remembered now what he'd allowed himself to forget in his need of her. He was a mutation, a freak of nature. He couldn't allow himself to reproduce.

His arms were locked around Alyssa's sweet body, his lips were against hers. It would be hell to let her go.

He gritted his teeth and gently pushed her back three inches.

"Can't do this," he said. "No protection at hand." And he started to rise and dress. Somehow he had to get her out of here without hurting her more than he already had by his lack of self-control.

"I already thought of that," she said softly, and her small hand splayed against his chest, shoving him back. Quickly she opened the packet she produced and lightly trapped him in her hands, unrolling the condom.

Her delicate fingers danced over him, and a roaring began in his head. When she positioned herself over him and lowered herself, his head fell back. He clutched her hips.

"Love me," she whispered fiercely.

He should say no. He should get the hell out of here.

"I will," he promised, as he gave in to his body's demands. He would love her, give her pleasure, and above all, he would do his best to make this good for her, since there wouldn't be another time for them.

With one swift move, he flipped her over. His hands and his lips found her, as he rocked within her and felt her heartbeat join with his. He caressed her and knew her and gave her all that he could ever give a woman.

He gave her more than he had ever given any woman. And knew that it was not enough.

But it was all that he was capable of.

As his hands joined with hers and he slid into her depths one more time, she cried out and he drank her sighs.

He plunged within her again and found pleasure and bliss and heaven. For once in his life he was there.

And he slept.

Two hours later Alyssa awoke and eased herself off the sofa, propping her elbows on her knees as she watched Connor sleep, his legs tangled in the afghan she had pulled over him.

He looked so satisfied, so peaceful, so boyishly handsome that she was almost overwhelmed by the need to touch him just to connect with him. But she knew that with Connor that would be unwise. He saw things other people didn't see, he felt things when his flesh met another human's. She might wake him.

And above all, she wanted to give him sleep.

It was the reason she had originally decided to make love to him, because she knew he wouldn't be able to escape the sleep that had obviously been eluding him for days. His eyes had been sunken, his expression haunted, his features gaunt. She'd wanted to give him rest.

Her good intentions had lasted about three seconds. The minute he'd placed his hands on her, she knew that her motives weren't nearly as unselfish as she'd wanted them to be.

And she didn't care. What Connor gave her when he touched her was incredible, remarkable. It was a once-in-a-century experience, and any woman would be a complete blockhead to walk away from that.

Still, the experience had totally blown her away. Watching him now, she was feeling all kinds of crazy, outlandish things. Things it wouldn't be wise to examine.

"You're going to freeze sitting on the floor."

She jumped when his gravelly voice broke into her thoughts, scattering them.

"Come here," he said, and reached down for her. "You need cover. I'll get up."

"No." She started to push him back, but he had already sat up and was reaching for his clothing.

She was not going to be the only one naked. Not now, now that reality was intruding.

Swiftly Alyssa slipped on her clothes. When she was fully dressed, she turned to him.

"We need to talk," she said.

"Yes." But something about his tone of voice told her that they weren't exactly speaking of the same thing.

"I know all about you and Jake." That was a lie. She only knew what Jake had been willing to share, and it was obvious that there were gaps in what he'd told her, but if she said that, Connor would retreat into his solitude. He would take on all the burdens of whatever was wrong himself.

That just wasn't going to fly with her.

"You know?" he said, and it was clear that he didn't believe her. "Then you know why I have to ask you to go back to the school and lock all the doors and keep the children safe. They are safe, aren't they?"

Guilt lay heavy in his tone. She knew what he was

thinking. While they'd been wrapped in each other's arms, something might have happened to the kids.

She touched his arm. "Mrs. Morrissey is there, and I asked her brother to come by and stay, as well. We're moving the children into the finished portion of the new building. At least it's more secure than the old one. If I need to, I'll hire guards. Do I need to?"

"I think so."

Anger rose up within her. What had Jake gotten him into?

"This has something to do with your missing family, doesn't it?"

"Go home, Alyssa. Take care of yourself and the children and wait until you hear from me. Don't come here again." He reached out and stroked her cheek.

Her throat nearly closed up. She knew he was going to close himself off again, and this time he wouldn't make it easy for her to get inside. He was never going to let her get near enough to touch him again.

The pain was so great that she knew this was something she needed to pay attention to. She was doing all the wrong things, getting involved where she had no business getting involved, letting herself feel things she should never have allowed herself to feel.

He was right. She should back out the door and run.

"You can tell me what's going on yourself," she said quietly, "or I can start asking a lot of questions in places that will attract attention. I know how much you love the media."

Connor swore beneath his breath.

"That wouldn't be good for the children."

"I wouldn't involve the children. This would be

strictly you and me. I'm used to dealing with reporters. I know how to pique their interest.''

A rough half smile flitted across his face and then disappeared. ''Is this how you hoodwink the children into doing what you want them to? The magic that gets five-year-old boys to eat their peas and carrots?''

''Sometimes a woman has to be ruthless.'' She hoped she sounded ruthless.

He tucked a finger beneath her chin.

She swallowed hard and tried to slow her heartbeat so that he wouldn't know just how scared she was.

''You're not as calm as you'd like me to believe.''

She lifted her head, and his thumb drifted lower, slicking against her sensitive flesh. ''No, I'm not,'' she whispered. ''But I'm desperate. I'm capable of quite a great deal, things that don't even begin to rate as wise, when I'm desperate.''

''You'd really go to the media?''

''If I thought it would make a difference.''

For five long seconds he held her there, his pulse and hers mingling.

''You're scared,'' he said quietly.

''I'm terrified.''

''I don't want you to be scared.''

''Then level with me. It's not the truth that hurts, but the not knowing. That's what frightens me most.''

He blew out a breath and collapsed on the couch. He drew her down beside him. ''All right. It's like this. Jake *is* my brother, I've decided that I'm sure of that. I've done some investigating of my own. But there's more than just Jake. Other brothers and sisters. More of us, and we're…not normal.''

And he proceeded to tell her the truth.

She sat quietly, listening to all he had to say.

"My brother Gideon," he finally said, "is like me. I have the same enhanced technological skills, the ability to see things in different ways than most people do. That means I might be better able to track him than other people would be. It gives me an edge."

"It puts you in harm's way."

"As it is, we're all in harm's way. I can't just sit by and do nothing if I can make a difference."

She took his hands in her own. "I understand."

"But I don't want you or the children to get caught up in this thing."

"I'm already caught up in it."

"No."

"Yes."

"I didn't hire you for this. Saving the owner of the Haven wasn't in your job description."

"You *are* the Haven. That makes you and all that affects you my business."

"Is this how you snowed the board? By being so pushy?"

She chuckled. "It's how I got you to keep me on for a trial basis, too, don't you remember?"

"I remember."

"I'm sorry, Connor, but I have to help when I can help."

"Then go back to the Haven. Bolt all the doors, close all the windows, lock yourself and the children away from the outside world. Protect them."

"I will. I'll make sure they have around-the-clock security, hire extra teachers so they're never alone and check up on the children every single day. I'll visit and make sure things are running smoothly, and I'll run your phone bill up to the heavens calling and talking to each and every one of them each day. But don't ask me to hide there with them. Right now I'm needed here."

"I have servants," Connor replied.

"Yes, and you intimidate them into doing anything you say. If you tell them you don't need food or sleep, they go along with that."

"I'm an adult, Alyssa. A fully grown man."

"I know that." Her voice was hoarse with emotion. "I know that so well. What's more, you're a genius, and you may well be the only one capable of finding Achilles, of finding Gideon. The world needs you to find him, and the children are a part of that world. To do that, you have to stay alert and healthy."

"I'm healthy."

"You're exhausted, and your nerves are frayed."

He started to slash his hand downward to argue, but she caught it between her own. She pressed his palm to her cheek. "I know that because I'm exhausted worrying about you, and my nerves are frayed. Don't send me away, Connor. I worry. I don't eat or sleep. Don't give me more days like the last few."

"Alyssa—"

"I know. That was manipulative, but it was also the truth. Let me stay. I can help you. I know tons about motivation and the human mind-body connection. That will make things move more quickly."

"Will you feed me spinach surprise?"

His rueful response drew a small shaky laugh from her. "Maybe."

He took her face in his palms. "This isn't smart."

"It's very smart. You have things you have to do. You can't be expected to concentrate on the little things that make life go on. But I can. I can make sure that while you're immersing yourself in the hunt for Gideon, you have the strength to do it and enough sleep to stay alert so that you don't miss anything. I can manage your household and your servants and still make sure that the school and the kids get all they need. It's what I do, Connor, and I'm good at it in the same way you're good at seeing mathematical and technological solutions to everyday problems."

"I know you are." He caught her by surprise by kissing her. "And I appreciate the woman that you are." He kissed her again. "You're so much more than I thought you were the day I first met you." He kissed the underside of her jaw.

"Thank you," she said primly.

"But running a school takes up all your time. It would be irresponsible of me to let you stay. You have to go back. You can see that, can't you?"

She clasped her hand over the spot that he'd just kissed, trying to absorb the tingling and the need that burned within her. She stood up suddenly.

"I can't believe you tried to use my own hormonal responses to you to get me to leave."

He shrugged. "If I told you I was enjoying it, would that make a difference?"

She blinked and gasped. "It most certainly would not," she said, even though she was secretly amused and, okay, thrilled that he hadn't strictly been using her.

"Anyway, it won't work. You can't sweet-talk me into leaving."

"Stubborn woman."

"Overbearing man."

"I knew I should have fired you when I had the chance." He sounded sincere. His words ripped through her like fire. The urge to turn and hide from the hurt was great, but this was Connor. He hid behind words, used them as weapons.

"You'll have to have me arrested if you want me out of your house. I'll wait." And she sat down again.

"Alyssa." His tone was low and deep and slow. He dropped to one knee beside her. "I don't want you in danger."

"I won't be. I'll be with you."

"And if something happened and I couldn't protect you, how would I feel?"

She knew what he meant. He was blind and that put him at a disadvantage now and then—but not most of the time. Most of the time he was capable of so much more than any other man she'd known. And besides, she didn't care. It wasn't her safety she was concerned about. He was the one chasing the bad guys.

"Your house is a fortress. I only got in because your housekeeper knew me. That's not going to happen again. We'll make sure it doesn't."

"Alyssa, go."

She looked around for the telephone, then handed it to him. "I'm trespassing. If you want me out of here, have me hauled away in handcuffs."

For half a second she thought he was going to do just

that. His expression grew dark. He scowled, looking like a volcano ready to blow.

"I'll take care of you," he finally said. "And heaven help me if I mess things up."

Connor dialed the number Jake had left him. At the sound of his brother's voice, finally convinced that Jake *was* his brother, he felt his emotions rise to near flood stage.

"You win," he finally said, his voice a harsh scrape of sound. "I believe you. I'll help you, but on one condition."

"Name it."

"I want extra security for my kids and for all of my employees, both at Solutions Unlimited and at Woodland Haven, especially for Alyssa. She'll be traveling back and forth between my house and the school. I don't want her to be a target."

"That's not a problem. I'll make sure she's covered by the best available. Your other employees and the children, too. I'll post extra guards around the perimeter of the school."

"I don't want the children to be scared."

"I'll handpick the guards. They'll be invisible, and they'll know that protecting the children from nightmares is also part of the job."

"Good. I'm glad you understand."

"I'm not married, just engaged, so I don't have children yet, but I know about responsibility and about worrying about others. Right now I feel as if I'm responsible for the fate of the world. Narrowing it down to a few children, some of whom I even caught glimpses of when I was at the Haven, makes it more personal. That's a good thing. I'll help you take care of them.''

Connor hoped he was right in trusting this man. He prayed he was not making a mistake in exposing everyone he cared about to a stranger offering promises.

''Good,'' was all he said. ''Let's get started on this as soon as possible. No point in wasting time. I need some information, a starting point.''

''You've got it. I'll bring you what I can.''

''Don't worry about having anything translated into braille. No point in involving more people than necessary. My scanner and computer will read to me whatever paperwork you have. If I have questions, I'll rely on you for the answers.''

''Anything you need, it's yours.''

''Thanks, but I've got everything I need for now. What I want is a starting point. You don't have one of those to give me, do you?''

''If I did, I might have left you alone.''

Connor didn't know what to make of that, so he ignored it.

''I'll get started as soon as we hang up,'' he promised.

''Just one question,'' Jake said.

''What?''

''I've been waiting several days. I would have sworn you were going to tell me to go to hell. What made you decide to help?''

That was an uncomfortable question. With an uncomfortable answer.

''You said that the world was at risk. I have people who depend on me, and I didn't want to fail them.''

''That habit of protecting others must rub off on your employees. I had a call from Alyssa.''

''She called you?''

''In a sense. She made darn sure I called her. Seems she wasn't happy about me. You've got someone pretty special there.''

Connor's hackles rose. ''You said *you* had someone?''

Jake laughed. ''Yes. Tara's lovely. I'm not after your Alyssa.''

Sure, Connor thought. His brother was probably the type who had a new fiancée every year. Alyssa's beauty had been reputed to make more than one man think about shedding a fiancée or wife. Despite those thoughts, he said, ''Right.

''And it wouldn't matter,'' he lied. ''But I wouldn't want my brother harassing my employees.''

''Wouldn't think of it. Is she there?''

Connor couldn't help turning toward Alyssa, who he knew was listening to his side of the conversation. ''Why do you ask?''

''I'd like to talk to her.''

Reluctantly Connor held the phone out to her.

''Seems you've made an impression on my brother. He wants to talk to you.''

Alyssa wondered at the scowl on Connor's face as she took the phone. ''Mr. Ingram?''

''Call me Jake.''

''All right…Jake.'' Was that a growl Connor had let slip? She looked at him. He was standing there, his feet braced apart, his hands clasped behind his back. It was clear he was not going to let this conversation be private.

"Was he all right when you found him?"

She didn't want to make Connor feel self-conscious. "As well as could be expected given how much had been going on."

"You mean how much I dumped on him all at once?"

"Yes. Exactly." She tried to sound cheerful for Connor's sake, but her cheerful tone only seemed to make Connor draw his brows together harder.

"This task he's taking on isn't going to be easy," Jake explained. "The Coalition has survived for several decades. The WBH took place back in April, and it's already November and I haven't located Achilles. Those in charge at the Coalition don't have Connor's special powers, but they're pretty brilliant in their own ways, and they have Gideon, who is a genius and who has had more than half a lifetime learning how to hide. This is going to take time, and it's going to be frustrating, even for someone of Connor's abilities."

"And as he gets closer to discovering their whereabouts, the pressure and—" she didn't want to use the word danger in front of Connor "—everything else increases." Including Connor's frustration and his sense of responsibility toward her and the kids.

"That's it, exactly."

"I see."

"I'd be there if I could, but there are other elements I need to see to right now. I'll check in when I can," Jake promised.

Alyssa half covered the phone with her hand. ''If I need to reach you?''

Connor reached out to take the phone from her hand. She danced away.

''Call this number,'' Jake said, calling off some figures. ''I'm leaving it with Connor, too. It's not direct, but I'll eventually find out and come running.''

''That's all I needed to hear.''

''I think Connor's a lucky man, Alyssa.''

''Things aren't that way,'' she said, reminding herself of that fact.

''Sorry to hear it. I'll talk to you later. I can't wait to meet both of you again under better circumstances.''

''Me, too,'' she said and her sigh was heartfelt. Things had just gotten many times more complicated than they had been a week ago, and they had been complicated enough at that time.

She gave the phone back to Connor, but as she did, she heard Jake tell Connor that he was glad to have found his brother. He wanted him to meet the rest of the family as soon as possible.

Connor nearly froze with the phone only halfway to his ear. ''I'll help you find Gideon,'' he said quietly. ''That's all I've agreed to.''

She didn't hear what Jake's answer was. And then Connor hung up the phone.

''Let's set down the ground rules,'' he said, looking at her.

Twelve

Connor scrubbed his hand back through his hair, trying to concentrate on the information Jake had given him. He'd been studying it for days. Lab reports, parts of Violet's diaries, notes Jake had scribbled himself. Information that had been gathered from his brothers and sisters. All of it relevant, none of it getting Connor any closer to where he needed to be.

"Damn it," he said, tearing the last paper from the scanner and dumping it on his desk. "This guy's a genius. How could he be so invisible?"

A light tap at the door and Drifter shifting against his shoes alerted Connor to Alyssa's presence. He knew it was her. That was the way she knocked, and Drifter didn't react that way to his housekeeper. Besides, pretty much everyone else stayed away these days. His servants were either avoiding him and his rough moods or Alyssa was keeping them away. For their benefit or his, he didn't know.

He heard the soft whoosh as she entered, the click of her heels as she moved toward him. The tray she pushed in front of him scraped on the desk. The aroma of tomato soup and melted cheese drifted to him. He loved tomato soup, and she knew it.

Connor frowned and tried to concentrate on some information regarding Gideon's early years.

"You have to eat sometime," she said.

"I will." He kept his voice gruff. He refused to let himself open to her. The more he'd delved into his family's history, the more he realized just how stained a man's past could be. This was a tale of ambition and greed, of choosing science over humanity, of manipulating people and DNA and discarding the wreckage. Much of it was ugly. He didn't want Alyssa touched by any of it. Moreover, he knew that she had volunteered to help him do the things she believed he could not always do for himself. See to the details. Because he was blind. She was caring for him as if he were a child.

Darkness overtook him in a way that blindness never had.

"Connor?"

"I'll eat it later." He shoved the tray aside.

The gesture felt childish. He knew she didn't think of him as a child. When they'd made love, they were every bit a man and a woman. But a man couldn't live in a woman's bed, and the world they inhabited saw him for what he was. How could she not? Still, he felt her hurt radiating through her stoic silence. He just couldn't do the smart thing and leave it.

"All right, I'll eat a little soup now," he conceded.

"I'm glad. You're not taking care of yourself properly."

"Maybe I don't need to. I've got a bossy woman taking me to task every time I fail to eat or take a nap." And he was doing his best to ignore her, not to let himself give in and touch her again. He was failing miserably.

"Sometimes bossy is helpful," she said, her voice laced with good humor. What kind of woman put up with a grump like himself and then put a smile in her voice the minute he eased up on her a bit?

A patient woman, an incredible woman. A woman he couldn't have.

He shoved too large a spoonful of soup in his mouth, and the heat seared him. It was all he could do not to spit the stuff out. No way was he doing that when she wanted him to eat it so badly. Besides, pain was good. It distracted him from her.

"I saw the children again today," she said. "They asked about you. I told them you were working on a new job. They understood."

He took another bite of soup to keep from answering. He knew as she did that the children didn't understand. How could any child understand abandonment for any reason? But she needed to believe that.

He wanted her to have what she needed.

"You can't go on like this much longer, Connor," she said, her voice strained. "You're pushing yourself too hard, day and night. You need rest."

"I'll get it when the job is done."

"Are you making any progress?"

He wished he could tell her yes. Instead he shook his head. "I'm working my way through back issues of newspapers for the past few years, looking for any slipup, any glitch, anything that might indicate that some mathematical genius is hiding in a cave somewhere. They've hidden him well."

"Or maybe he's hidden himself. I know a man like that, one who has extreme talent but plays it down."

She had edged in close, and he swallowed the groan. He forced himself to put down the bowl he was holding and to grasp the arms of his chair. Hard.

"A man who could mastermind the World Bank Heist doesn't think like other men," he said, doing his best not to reach out and touch her. He wanted nothing more than to pull her onto his lap, breathe in the scent of her hair, lose himself in her softness. "Making money disappear in a flash through a series of complex computer transfers that most people couldn't even begin to fathom? How many men could engineer such a scenario? And yet Achilles did, and in doing so, he tilted the world on its axis, turned things to chaos. He's a rare and crafty man, and more than that, he has accomplices who have committed heinous acts. They've murdered people."

His voice was raw and he couldn't hide that from her.

"I know."

But she didn't. Not really.

"Alyssa, this man, this kind of man, is my brother. He's my genetic twin in many ways."

"He's nothing like you." She moved even closer, pressing her body against his side as she clutched his arm.

But he was. Gideon had been the abandoned son, the one Violet had left with the Coalition just the way Henry had left him at the Haven. She hadn't been able to save him, but Gideon wouldn't know that. He would only know that he had been left behind. And being deserted by the ones who should care changed a person, wrecked him for real relationships.

Connor knew something of how Gideon would think, how he would react. He could almost sympathize with the man, except lives were at stake here.

"He's me," he insisted, drawing strength from the conviction that he had a job to do. "I just have to go with that. I've got to stop running from that and sink into it. Then I'll know what he might do, where he would go."

"Connor?" Alyssa's voice was laced with concern. "Don't go that route. Don't try to get into his head so deeply. This could hurt you." She touched his brow and he turned his chair, lifting her onto his lap.

Idiot of a man, Connor thought, knowing he shouldn't be touching her this way. It only complicated things. He could tell she was worried because she thought he couldn't take care of himself. He'd lived with that all of his life. People grabbing his arm to drag him across streets, people stepping in to do the things he had sweated and struggled to learn for himself. He had toiled through endless repetitions to teach himself survival skills. He could cook if he needed to; he could even work with wood and power tools. He could ski down mountains. And yet his father had thrown him away, just as his former fiancée had been unable to deal with his blindness. It killed him that Alyssa might think him weak and flawed, as well.

"Nothing can hurt me," he said.

She gave a sound of distress, and Connor sank his hand into her hair, binding her to him as he bent over her lips.

"You make me crazy with your worrying," he whispered.

"I can't help it."

"I know." Because he couldn't help worrying about her, either. "For now let's not worry." He kissed her once, hard, then rose with her in his arms and made his way into the adjoining room, his bedroom. Dropping her onto the feather mattress, he followed her there, trapping her with his lips and with his arms. She reached up for him and pushed aside the open neck of his shirt, laying her lips on his skin, brushing back and forth.

He nearly fell apart, but he held on to his control. And he swore he would end this soon. This insane need of her, this taking when he should let go and walk away. This risky behavior. Just as soon as he found Gideon he would take care of things with Alyssa, disentangle her from his life. Because with every new thing he discovered about his past and his family, he realized that he could not ever drag a woman into that morass of mistakes and flaws. And he couldn't ask her what he had once asked another woman, to change her life to accommodate his special circumstances. He couldn't have Alyssa Fielding. Someday soon he would have to decide what he would do about that, ask her to leave the Haven or leave it himself.

No question, he would be the one leaving.

But not yet. For tonight he was just a man and she was his woman. Genetics didn't matter and in the dark, neither did sight.

Tonight he would be gloriously selfish. Tomorrow was soon enough for regrets and goodbyes.

* * *

Alyssa looked down at Connor as he began to stir. For the first time in days he looked slightly rested, though the stress still showed on his face.

"Maybe you should have told Jake no," she said, framing his face with her hands.

"And what would he do then?"

"Find someone else?"

"Who?"

She sighed. "I know you're right. Who better to find Gideon than you? But I don't want you to be this way."

He sat up in bed and ran a restless hand down her shoulder and arm, finally catching her hand in his own. "I am this way, Alyssa. I've always been this way."

"I don't mean your genius."

"I know. You mean my obsession, the fact that I catch hold of something and lose myself in it, refusing food or rest. It's all a part of the same thing, though, you know. It's who and what I am, like the blindness. It sets me apart from the world."

He was giving her a warning. She knew he was. Pain hit at her heart and she couldn't deny that she was falling in love with him, even though she'd known from the start that this would be a one-sided relationship. He could want her body, but he couldn't or wouldn't love her.

She fought against the inevitable.

"You're not apart. You have family now."

He chuckled, a sound with no humor and plenty of scorn. "Not a family like any other, I'd wager. We're misfits, every one, but even there, Alyssa, I'm different. I don't fit. There's no future there."

"But Jake—"

He held up one hand. "I've talked to Jake several times in the past week. He's made his arguments."

"I've talked to him, too. He seems like a good, sincere man."

Connor stiffened. "I suppose he does. I can't fault him for hanging back, anyway."

"He wishes he could do more for you."

"I wish I could end this sooner rather than later. I don't like the situation I've placed you in. Whenever you travel back and forth between here and the Haven, I worry."

She leaned back in his arms and shook her head, her curls sliding against his chest. "Don't worry about me. I'm fine. It's you I'm concerned about. If you get too close to them…"

"Then we'll have them," he said, tightening his grip on her. "Then I'll stop worrying and life can go on as it was before Jake arrived."

Except she knew that that wasn't true. Even making love to her tonight, Connor was withdrawn. He was slowly pulling away from her, and she couldn't do a thing to protect herself or her heart.

Maybe he'd been right from the first. She shouldn't have come to the Haven. It would hurt him to hurt her.

And he would hurt her. There was no way that he could keep from it.

But she would do her best to keep him from knowing of her pain. He was already a man who blamed himself for too much.

Her broken heart was not going to be on Connor Quinn's conscience if she could help it.

* * *

Jake had just gotten off the phone with Alyssa. What a classy lady she was. He wondered if his dear brother knew just what a gem he had in her.

Alyssa was making sure Connor didn't kill himself from neglect while he worked on finding Gideon. She traveled back and forth between Connor's house and the Haven and made sure that every kid got his bit of quality time with her. She had them tape little messages to Connor and insisted that he send back tapes in reply.

She cooked and coddled and fussed and forced her will on anyone who didn't do the right thing.

And she didn't seem even slightly fazed by the fact that the man she was sleeping with had turned out to be a genetic mutation or that his entire family was similarly affected and that one of his siblings was a fugitive responsible for turning the world upside down and crazy.

If Alyssa could handle all that he and Connor had thrown at her in the past week, maybe there was hope for him and Tara, too. He should have leveled with her a long time ago.

What had he been waiting for? A sign?

"Well, looks like you've got one," he muttered to himself. "Alyssa took on a job as director of Woodland Haven and ended up caught in the WBH mess. And she's handling it, she's keeping quiet about things that can't be revealed, and her attitude toward Connor hasn't changed."

Well, not exactly. If anything, Alyssa was worrying about his brother more every day. She was clearly a woman with a bad case of almost-in-love illness.

Tara had been a faithful friend and fiancée, hadn't

she? She loved him, didn't she? It was wrong for a man to keep his future wife in the dark.

Time to turn on the lights and reveal his secrets.

Jake waited for Tara to say something, anything.

She folded her arms over her chest, but he could still see that her fingers were shaking against her white silk suit. "You're telling me that you're some sort of genetically engineered man with superhuman powers?" Her eyes flashed angry sparks.

"I'm telling you that, yes, I'm a bit different."

"You're the result of an experiment?"

"That's not exactly the way I'd put it, but basically you're right about that. But I am flesh and blood, Tara. I'm a man, the same man you've always known."

"And you're on a mission to save the world."

"I have a job to perform, one I'm uniquely suited for."

"Because there are more of you. You're not the only one." Her voice broke slightly. She turned away.

Jake sighed and moved toward her. At the sound of his footsteps she scooted away farther.

"I should have told you sooner," he said softly.

She whirled, her face mirroring her distress. "You should have. A long time ago. I've been making plans, Jake. I had my life all set. I just wanted an ordinary life with an ordinary wealthy man. You knew that."

He hadn't. Not completely.

"Love wasn't a part of the equation?"

"Love is the result of two like-minded people, two people with similar backgrounds, growing together over time." She raised her chin defiantly.

"What are you saying, Tara?" His voice was so much calmer than he would have expected it to be, given the circumstances and the dread that was rising within him.

"I'm saying that I thought we wanted the same things. I thought we were alike. We're not. I see that now. I don't want to save the world, Jake. I don't want a superhero that the tabloids are going to rip into if they ever find out the truth. In the circles where I want to travel, they would definitely find out the truth. It's not the life I dreamed of."

No, he could see that it wasn't. She had always been big on appearances. It must be disappointing to find out that he had secrets lurking beneath the surface.

"Call me weak, Jake, but I don't want that kind of life."

He closed his mind to whatever thoughts were lurking there. Later he would deal with them. "Then you don't have to have it."

She nodded and looked daggers at him. "Matt and Carey's wedding is next week. I have my dress, and I thought we were going to go together, but now that's the last thing I want. Please don't come and please don't try to see me again."

He flinched at that. She was leaving him. Moreover, this wasn't a simple thing she was asking. He'd known Matt since college. Staying away on the happiest day of his friend's life would sting, but he supposed Tara knew that. He only hoped Matt would understand and forgive him.

"All right," he agreed.

"You should have told me sooner," she repeated.

"Yes, I guess I should have." He stepped close to kiss her goodbye, but she merely shook her head and bolted for the door. "I'm sorry" was on his lips, but he never got a chance to say the words.

Connor wondered what had brought his brother here in person to check up on things. They had spoken several times in the past week, but only over the telephone.

"I'm beginning to feel as if I have a greater idea of what makes a man like Gideon tick," Connor said. "There's a bond there that I can't deny."

"Even though you want to?" Jake asked.

Connor's fingers froze on the paperweight he'd picked up off his desk. "Meaning what?"

"Meaning that we're different from the rest of the world. It sets us apart, sometimes scares people away."

Exactly the kind of thing that Connor was trying not to think about these days, but something in Jake's voice alerted him that he wasn't just waxing philosophical.

"You sound like you speak from experience."

Jake let out an exasperated laugh, more like a bark really. "I just finally told my fiancée the truth about who and what I am. She didn't take it well. Said she didn't want to be married to a genetically engineered superhero."

Pain slid through Connor. He knew that feeling, and now he shared it. With his brother. Without thinking, he rose from his chair and rounded the desk.

"Must be tough being the guy who heads up the investigation of the World Bank Heist. The old lonely-at-the-top scenario."

"You know it's not the fact that I'm the one in charge of the investigation that made the difference."

He knew. They were mutations, not like other people.

"I just wanted to give you a new number to reach me at," Jake continued. "I'm flying out to visit with Gretchen. She and her husband are expecting a baby, and I like to check in on her now and then."

His sister was going to have a baby? The very thought bothered Connor.

"Tell her…congratulations," Connor said, but he couldn't see how anything good could come of someone like himself or one of his siblings reproducing.

"I'll tell her. When this is over, you'll have to meet Gretchen, Faith and Marcus."

"Maybe then," Connor agreed, but he didn't think so. This conversation with Jake had left him thinking one thing, something he'd known all along. Some people were meant to be alone. In his case, it went beyond the difficulties in trusting and forming lasting relationships. For a man like himself, with the dual challenge of being a Protean and a blind man, asking a woman to share his world was impossible.

This conversation had solidified one thought. He wasn't going to have a life with Alyssa. For her sake, he needed to break off all contact. Besides, right now he had places to go where she couldn't follow. Sitting here in his house, he wasn't making the kind of progress he needed to make, and there was no way he was going to allow her to put herself into the line of fire.

"I think I'm going to have to step up the investigation," Connor said. "I may need to move around the country a bit."

"I'll make sure that your back is covered."

Connor nodded. "I appreciate it. And I'd also appreciate it if you'd make sure that whoever is guarding Alyssa keeps an eye on her and reassures her that my needs are being seen to. I'm not sure she'll believe me on that one and I don't want her showing up anyplace where she might be in harm's way."

"Not a problem."

Good. Maybe if he got away and poured his heart into this investigation, he could begin forgetting about Alyssa. That would make the eventual break that much easier.

For now he had to make some plans.

He had a brother to catch. And a woman to wipe out of his heart.

Jake was getting ready to leave. "About Alyssa," he said.

Connor froze. "What?"

"Something came to my attention today. It's probably nothing, but…"

Connor waited for his brother to speak.

Thirteen

Alyssa felt a sense of dread as Connor came into the room. There was no smile on his face, no welcome in his expression. That alone wouldn't have alerted her that there was a problem, but the fact that he was seeking her out when she'd been the one force-feeding him for the past week had her knock-kneed nervous.

"You wanted something?" she asked. Like my heart? The fact that she was all too eager to serve it up to him with willing hands sent waves of anxiety through her.

"Come sit down," he said.

"Oh, no, I'm fine." She pretended to fuss with a vase of flowers she'd already arranged.

"What's wrong?" His voice was gentle. "I hear you fidgeting."

She placed her hands behind her back. "I guess I'm just wondering what the kids are up to." Which wasn't a lie, since she was always wondering what they were up to.

"That's good, then, because it goes along with my plan."

"Plan?" He had a plan that involved her and the children? That should have been good. She could tell by his too-calm manner that it wasn't good. This was a man who had been tearing his hair out all week looking for a solution to the puzzle of his brother. And who wasn't eating or sleeping and was worrying about her and the kids constantly. If he had found Gideon, he would be more than calm. He'd be ecstatic, and he definitely wasn't that. Instead he simply looked determined.

"What's your plan?" The words came out a little strained, a little too soft.

"You've been a help to me during this past week, more than a help, but…"

"But?" She tried to keep the dread from her voice.

"Alyssa, from here on out it's anyone's guess what will happen. I've covered all the data on the WBH. I'm searching databases of information on former grads of the top schools and the top minds in the mathematical community, but I haven't come up with anything, and it's time to up the tempo of the investigation. I'm going to go out in the field and start turning over rocks and see what's under them. When I get hold of a good lead, I may be leaving at a moment's notice, moving around a lot. Thank you for all your help and for your concern, but I've spent my life managing on my own. I can do that again, but the children can't manage without you. It's time for you to go back to the Haven."

Alyssa's head was throbbing with sudden pain, but somehow she found her backbone. "And if you go off chasing Gideon, who goes with you?"

"One of Jake's bodyguards." His voice was sure and certain.

She felt like an ice statue. "May I ask what brought

this on?'' Please, don't say you're already tired of me, her heart cried out.

"Several things. Jake told me someone followed you the other day. And I talked to Edwina today and she said it happened again this afternoon."

"They were reporters."

"Maybe, but that only made it clear to me just how many risks you've taken lately. How many I've allowed you to take. I won't do that anymore. You're not staying."

"Oh?" What could she say to that? How could she argue? And shouldn't she be happy about the fact that he would be protected?

"A bodyguard isn't going to make sure you eat properly and get enough sleep."

"I'm a fully grown man, Alyssa. I don't need a keeper."

Or anyone else. She knew that was what he wanted to say.

"I'll take you back," he said.

"That won't be necessary. I've been doing fine on my own for the past week. The reporters didn't bother me. In fact, they've been a great excuse for the security guards at the Haven. I've told them and the children that the guards are there to keep out the press."

"I said I'll take you back."

"And then what?"

"I'll devote myself to my quest. I'll find him. Then it will be done."

The finality in his voice was like a sledgehammer to her heart. She knew that he wasn't just referring to his search for his brother. Her month was drawing to a close. He had decided that she was good for the Haven, but he hadn't counted on what had happened between them. And that negated everything. Connor Quinn wouldn't marry and he wouldn't carry on a long-term affair with the director of the Haven. She supposed she had known that from the day she'd stepped into his bed. Getting physically involved with him had been a mistake.

And yet it hadn't. She wouldn't have given that up for anything.

"I'll pack my things," she said quietly.

Alyssa couldn't remember much of the next few minutes. She supposed she threw everything she'd brought with her into a bag. She had obviously climbed into the limo beside Connor while Drifter rode in his carrier.

All she really knew was that the car was carrying her back to the children, but away from Connor. Which was a darn good thing, she told herself. She was hired to care for the children, not to fall in love with her employer.

The miles passed with both Connor and herself silent, so silent that Drifter's breathing could be heard.

Alyssa braced herself for the moment when they would arrive. They'd called Mrs. Morrissey, and the children were certain to come out to greet them.

She would have to smile and be happy. Children should never suffer for the mistakes of adults. No one knew that better than she.

So when the car stopped, she allowed Connor to take her hand, trying not to feel too much. She tugged her hand free as soon as her feet touched the ground. Immediately he released her.

"Connor! Connor!" Joey came running up and hugged Connor around the waist. "We missed you!" Alyssa watched the eager boy's eyes light up at the sight of this man, the first person who had offered him stability.

"You're back!" Letice wheeled up as the others gathered around.

Connor smiled down at Joey and Letice. He ruffled Joey's hair, then released him as he dropped to one knee by Kanika's and Petra's sides. He reached out, touching each child, making contact, letting them know that he cared.

"I can't stay," he said simply. "Even though I'd like to. There's work I have to do. Something very important."

"Important?" Bud asked, stubbing his toe against a pile of snow.

Alyssa knew what he meant. So did Connor by the look of him.

"Not more important than you," he said sternly. "It's just something that has to be done. I'm afraid I can't explain."

"Don't need to," Bud said. "All those guys hanging around the place. Someone's trying to steal the ideas for our new place, aren't they? Trying to slip in and take pictures so that they can sell your ideas. That's what it is, isn't it? Someone's trying to mess with us and you're taking care of it, aren't you?"

So close and yet so far away, Alyssa thought, marveling at how a child's mind worked.

And then she thought it again as Connor reached out to touch her, then froze, letting his hand drop to his side. So close and yet so far away.

"Even if someone was to try to mess with us, you would never need to worry," Connor agreed. "I would be on it."

"But if you needed help, I would be it," Bud declared.

Connor traced one finger down Bud's cheek. You're a credit to the Haven, Bud."

"I am?"

"Definitely."

"That's me. A credit." Bud turned and bowed deeply and dramatically to the other children, who laughed. Alyssa automatically leaned near Connor and quietly explained about the bow.

"Thank you," he said, his voice far too polite.

"Alyssa will be here, and I'll leave messages with her. All of you help her, all right?"

"Yes, Connor. Will you be coming back to visit us longer soon?"

"As soon as I can."

"Good," Letice said, tugging on his hand. "Because we like you and you like us, too, don't you?"

For several seconds Connor didn't speak. Then he cleared his throat. "I like you all very much."

The stress apparent in his voice worried Alyssa. "For the short time Connor is here, why don't we all spend some time outside and play. Joey, you get the football, okay?"

Connor opened his mouth. To object and say that he

had to get going, she was sure. "Just for a few minutes," she pleaded. "They've missed you."

"I've missed them, too. More than you know." But he was wrong. She could tell by the way he relaxed just a bit that this was home for him. Of course he'd missed it horribly. And when Joey came running back with the football that beeped so that everyone could participate, Connor knelt beside him and asked if he'd played any good Monopoly games lately. He touched the little boy's cheek, and something passed between the two of them that told her this week separate from the children had cost Connor greatly, too. This thing with Gideon was costing him dearly. Suddenly he was trying to save everyone, especially her and the children.

The darn man just wouldn't admit that sometimes he needed saving a little bit, too. He needed some down time. "Are you ready to get trounced, Connor?" she asked teasingly.

Connor chuckled. "All right, madame director, you're on. You wanted to play. You start." He casually tossed her the ball. She missed.

"Uh-oh, looks like Alyssa isn't any better at football than she was at making snowballs," Petra said as the ball rolled away and Bud ran to retrieve it.

"Then why did she suggest it?" someone asked.

"Silly. Because she's a good sport, right, Connor?" Kanika asked. "She plays what she thinks we want to play."

Connor turned her way. "She is an excellent sport, in every way."

Alyssa's heart filled at the warmth in his voice, but

just then the entrance alarm sounded loudly, its shrill shrieks piercing the air.

"Drifter, come," Connor yelled, just as Alyssa started to run toward the entrance. "Alyssa, see to the children." He moved toward the building.

He's unarmed, was all Alyssa could think.

But one of Jake's guards passed her right then, and the children, frightened, clustered around her. She gathered them close. "This way," she said. She called to one of the security guards who was running toward the building, too. "Take care of them. Keep them safe," she said to the guard. "Stay with him," she told the children.

As soon as she was sure that everyone was going to do as they were told, she whirled and raced toward the Haven. At the entrance, Connor was in conversation with one of Jake's guards. As she approached, her breathing labored and loud, he raised his head.

"It's all right," he said. "Or reasonably so." Concern laced his voice.

"The intruder?"

He shook his head. "A new man on the security force, a replacement for one who had to take personal leave. We failed to key him into the system."

Alyssa knew heads would roll on that one.

"I'll talk to the staff," she said. "It's my fault. I should have been here to take care of it."

"You're here now, and anyway, I helped train the staff. I'll tend to it."

And that would be just one more thing he had to worry about. She moved closer, so that she was toe-to-

toe with him. "I'm the director, Mr. Quinn," she whispered. "It's my job. Let me do it."

It was as though she'd stuck a pin in an inflatable raft. Some of the stress eased out of him. He reached out as if to touch her.

"You are the director, and you do your job well. I'll back off."

"Good." But in truth, she wished he would move closer rather than backing off. And that was too darn bad.

She turned so that she could see the children. "It's all right, just a false alarm," she said.

But then she pivoted back toward Connor.

"The system worked," she said quietly. "It did just what it was supposed to do. That should make you feel happier about our safety."

"It does." But he sounded anything but happy. Instead he squatted down beside the area where the sensors were located. "Clever little device, isn't it? Sam here tells me that the info collected on the new man is very precise. Better than his own mother could give us."

Still, he frowned. "I have to leave."

Alyssa touched his arm. "May I speak to you first?"

"Of course." And he walked away with her to a spot where no one could hear.

"It works, Connor. We'll be fine."

"I don't like leaving you alone, but…"

"But what?"

"What good would I have done, anyway? A blind man can't chase a criminal. Do you know how it makes me feel to know that I couldn't have saved you if there had been someone here who posed a danger?''

She ignored the warning that told her not to touch him again. She placed her palm on his chest.

"You don't have to be all things, Connor."

"But there are some things that I need to be and do. I need to ensure your safety."

"And you have. You've provided us with the best technology money can buy."

"Technology wouldn't have stopped him."

"It might have. The doors locked, didn't they?"

"You were outside! They locked you out, as well."

"An oversight. I'm sure with that wonderful mind of yours, you'll come up with a solution, should such a thing ever happen again."

"You're damn right I will. And today, too."

She placed her other palm on his chest. "See, Connor, you take care of us. So well."

"Not well enough. Never well enough," and he gathered her against him and kissed her hard. Then he called to Drifter and got into his limo. Before she could recover from his unexpected embrace, he was gone.

Alyssa wondered when she would see him again and knew she had to protect her heart from what was coming.

He had been right that first day after all, and the board had been wrong. She was not the right person for this job, because, much as she loved it, she had gotten in too deep. If she had let Connor hire someone else, she wouldn't be heading for heartbreak right now.

When her trial here was up, it was all too clear what was going to happen.

But she couldn't think about that now.

She had children who needed her and a staff to supervise.

Her heart would just have to suffer through.

Connor rubbed his hands over his jaw and shook his head, warding off thoughts of Alyssa. He couldn't even begin to try to sleep. If he did, she would be there in his dreams. Her scent would surround him. The sound of her voice would make him claw the bed, fighting to keep from going to her. The memory of her touch—

He slammed his hand down on the desk and papers went flying.

"Get coffee. Get back to work," he muttered, standing up to stretch and to think.

Think about Gideon, he ordered himself. Where was Gideon now? What was he doing? What had a man of his talents been doing for the past twenty-plus years?

"Not vegetating. Not possible," he said. He knew that from experience. The numbers, the solutions wouldn't leave him alone. Usually it was a blessing. For a man in hiding it might have been a necessity, simply for sanity's sake.

And what would Gideon have done with his gifts, his blessing? Connor asked himself. He'd already been over and over the possibilities this past week before he'd sent Alyssa away, but the few times he'd come up with what appeared like a lead, it always ended in a dead end. He'd searched the aerospace industry. Too public. The computer fields. Too tight-knit and cutthroat.

He'd wondered how a man like Gideon could just drop off the face of the earth. His keepers must have wanted to hide him away very badly. Or maybe Gideon wanted to be hidden. After all, he had no family that he knew of, and if he had glimmerings of memory, they would be of abandonment, of being left alone.

He'd surely lose himself in the one thing that always stayed true and constant: his gifts.

Which were?

Like his own. Connor couldn't help wondering what his brother was like, if they shared other things beside their skills.

That wasn't good. Wanting to share was dangerous. It made a man vulnerable.

But a woman could be vulnerable, too. She could be hurt. He couldn't help wonder what Alyssa was doing right now. He'd grown too used to having her near, within hearing and touching distance.

Connor dropped onto the couch. He sank his hands into Drifter's fur.

"I should never have started anything with her. I'm afraid I hurt her, boy," he said. "I let her come here, I took her softness and then I sent her away. If I were her, I'd hate me right now, don't you think? I certainly left her abruptly enough, standing alone outside the entrance to the Haven. Just her and the machines, the ones she marveled at so much. She must hate them now. They must remind her of how I took her and then rejected her."

He couldn't help remembering her story of how potential parents had come to the orphanage where she'd been, always ignoring her, leaving her. Years of modeling and male adulation of her gorgeous body couldn't wipe that out.

And he'd been no better than those men.

His only consolation, a very small consolation, was that at least he knew she was perfectly safe now. The machines had worked, the guards had come running. When she'd been here with him, he'd worried constantly. No matter how secure the system or how many guards, nothing could make him forget that he was looking for a man who communed with killers, and that she was in danger just by being near him. If something had happened, if he hadn't been able to protect her, well...

Never mind, he told himself. It didn't matter now. She was away from him. The heat and attention would be off her, and with Jake's guards and the Haven's security systems, she'd be protected.

He almost managed to smile, remembering how she'd jumped when the alarm had gone off that day he'd taken her on a tour of the new facilities. She'd gotten him to open up about his passion, his inventions.

But the security system, though pure genius, wasn't his. He'd told her that.

It wasn't his.

He'd told her that, and yet...

It wasn't his, but it was someone's. Someone with vision and abilities beyond the norm. Someone special and different, he thought, remembering all the information that little contraption had given them today.

And what had been bothering him all afternoon, what he'd been holding at bay, came rushing back.

He'd known it, but he hadn't wanted to believe it. It was too eerie, too close at hand, too much as if he'd been manipulated. The thought that he could have bought into a security system invented by his missing brother, whom he was pursuing, was too much like a creepy coincidence.

''Or maybe not. Two mathematical minds are bound to veer toward each other, aren't they?''

He remembered telling Alyssa that the inventor of the device wouldn't be any ordinary man or woman. He had to examine it.

No, he didn't. He'd already done that, and he knew. This was a path he had to follow.

Connor sat down at his computer, tapped into the Internet and did a search into Redcom Systems. They had a very ordinary, very simple site. Much more simple than one would expect for a company that could produce the Haven's system. The site had very few graphics he had to circumnavigate, which told him that little time or effort had been put into it. Not much information, either.

For a second he almost wondered why they even had a site, if they weren't going to promote themselves beyond the norm. But of course, not having a site these days could send up a red flag in itself. Better to have one and keep it low-key.

Anyway, although the site netted no new information, it confirmed that their contact information hadn't changed since he'd purchased his system. That was really all he needed, anyway.

From here on out, he was in virgin territory. He was a man of numbers and technology, not a man who knew how to hunt. But only a man like himself could investigate Redcom and tell if there was potential there for hiding the mastermind of the WBH.

Quickly, he dialed the number and set up an appointment. He didn't bother giving a bogus name. As a former customer, he was probably already in their system, and that might work in his favor. All Redcom needed to believe was that he was a customer who had some follow-up questions about the product he'd purchased before buying them on a larger scale.

All he needed to do was get in the door and attempt to work a miracle by asking to speak to the man who created the magic at Redcom Systems.

But first he had to let Alyssa know he was going. It was only right.

And he just couldn't leave without hearing her voice once more.

Alyssa took the telephone receiver Mrs. Morrissey handed to her. She already knew it was Connor. She hoped that her hand wasn't shaking noticeably. She gave Mrs. Morrissey an apologetic look, then turned her back.

"Don't worry, dear. You can have privacy," the woman said with a chuckle as she tiptoed away.

"Alyssa?" Connor's voice was as deep as she remembered, as welcome.

"Are you all right?" She had to know. It had only been hours since she'd seen him, but they had been long hours.

"I'm fine." But he sounded tired. "I just wanted to let you know that I would be gone for a couple of days. I think I may have found him. At least I hope so."

"Where?"

"I'm not going to tell you that. It's probably better that you don't know."

"You'll tell Jake?"

"I have to. He's sending one of his watchdogs with me."

"Good. How do you feel about this? About being on the verge of finding your brother?"

The silence settled in. "I'm not sure. I've got mixed feelings. This isn't a family reunion I'm headed to."

But it was in a way. Gideon shared so many things with Connor, and not just the genetic makeup. This was going to be so difficult for Connor emotionally. Meeting with a brother for the first time in a bid to stop him from his illegal activities would be difficult for any man. How much more so would it be if that man had also been raised an outcast from his family?

And what if Gideon meant to harm Connor?

She wanted above all else to offer to come with him, but he was right about the children. She couldn't leave them, and besides, she knew that he wouldn't want her along. Begging him to take her would only make her appear pathetic and needy. She'd done enough of that in her teens. As an adult, she'd learned to know what a man wanted of her and never to suggest more.

"Connor?"

"Yes?"

"Take two bodyguards. Maybe three."

She half expected him to laugh. He didn't.

"I'll be fine, Alyssa. I promise. I told the kids I'd be back. I'll come for them," he said as he told her good-bye and hung up.

He would come for the children, but not for her.

She had the feeling that he wasn't going to be nearly careful enough.

She wanted to call Jake, to beg him to make sure Connor came home safely.

But if she did that, what would Connor think? How would he feel?

She didn't have to ponder very long. The fact that he was incapable of chasing down the perceived intruder this afternoon had singed his pride. Could she hurt him like that?

Could she bear it if something happened to him and he never came home or he came home injured?

"Aargh!" she screamed to the walls. "I hate sitting and waiting. I've spent too much of my life sitting and waiting." For someone to come and adopt her, for the world to accept her for what she was, not what she appeared to be. For someone to love her. The right someone.

Well, she'd met the right someone, and he wouldn't have her, even though he wanted her.

The rules were all crazy, anyway. The only important rule was that a person had to help those they loved if they could.

She picked up the phone and called Jake.

Fourteen

Jake listened as Alyssa explained the situation. "Don't you dare let anything happen to him," she said.

"He's my brother, Alyssa."

"I know that, but still..."

"I'll send all the help he'll allow. Will that make you feel better?"

"Nothing will make me feel good about this, but yes, that will help a little."

"Got it bad, don't you, kid?"

She ignored his comment. She'd spent too much time running from the inevitable to let someone else throw it up to her.

"Jake?"

"Yes, Alyssa."

"If you ever tell Connor that I called you and asked you to protect him, I'll deny every word. I'll tell him that you're not only his brother, you're a liar."

"I don't interfere in my brothers' personal lives."

"I know. You just want to make sure that one of them doesn't destroy life as we know it."

"And I want to have a chance to get to know Connor."

"Me, too," she said sadly.

"Don't worry, I'll guard him well," he told her. "And I won't tell him."

* * *

"So we're expecting a visitor? A potential buyer? And not just any buyer. Connor Quinn, a blind man who was raised in an orphanage." Agnes Payne paced the floor.

"What do you think he wants?" Oliver asked.

"Well, we know that he's one of the few people who have one of the prototypes for the Redcom 7000. Maybe this is just a service call." Agnes's voice was laced with cynicism. "Or maybe he wants to reminisce about his father and find out how he ended up in that orphanage."

"Which would be a good question. I didn't think Bloomfield was so sentimental, at least not until later. Thought maybe he'd even done away with the kid, which would have been a good thing."

"Now we have to deal with the results of Henry's sloppy sentimentality. Again."

"We could use this one if he's as good as Achilles."

Agnes scowled at him. "We never had control over this one. That makes him dangerous. And if we attempted to use blackmail, he'd be doubly dangerous. You can bet Ingram has him covered. What we have to do is get rid of him."

"If the genetic engineering took, he won't be that easy to fool."

"Then we do the next best thing."

"Which would be..."

"We disappear. We go even deeper than we already are. The man may be a genius, but he's blind. He has limitations."

"And we do not. What we've got is Achilles, which trumps a blind brother, even one with a brain designed by Henry Bloomfield."

"The man doesn't have a chance. Let's get to work. I think I know what to do."

Connor listened to the receptionist's directions over the phone. There was a paved half-mile lane leading up to Redcom Systems, which was located on a forested mountainside outside the town of Redemption, Oregon. The business itself was surrounded by a chain-link fence, with a security guard at a gatehouse where visitors had to check in.

"Of course," he said, "if I'm going to invest more money in something as expensive as the Redcom 7000, I'll want to speak to the inventor. I own one already, but if I'm going to purchase another, I'll want to know if any modifications have been made, so I'll have a number of questions."

"Of course, Mr. Quinn. The man you want would be Jonathan Desworth. Mr. Desworth will be available at three this afternoon. Will that suit your purposes?"

"Admirably," he said, then he took down the last bit of information and concluded the conversation. And it would give him a bit of time to look up whatever he could find about Jonathan Desworth. Connor tried not to let his anticipation build. Was Jonathan Desworth really Gideon? How did he feel about the possibility of meeting the man who had been engineered to take his place?

"Off kilter," he decided. He needed balance, an anchor. The desire to call Alyssa and share this with her was almost overwhelming. She had been there with him when he'd met Jake. She had done her best to aid him in this search. She should be here now.

And maybe if she were, she'd be in danger.

But the very ordinariness of the phone call, the receptionist's matter-of-fact attitude set off a sense of unease. Something wasn't right here. It didn't feel like danger exactly. It just felt like a dead end.

Maybe this was a stone with nothing beneath it. Perhaps he was chasing smoke.

And maybe by three o'clock he'd be looking at the mastermind behind the World Bank Heist. He had better get to work doing his research.

What was going on? Alyssa wondered that same morning. Jake had told her nothing, and she hadn't asked, although she was sure he and Connor had discussed the matter. Maybe Connor was simply trying to protect her by keeping her in the dark, or maybe he didn't trust her completely. Either way, he was right. The fewer people who knew, the safer he would be.

"Alyssa, you're not listening." She looked down to find Joey tugging on her hand. "I was reading you *Chicka Chicka Boom Boom,* and you didn't come in on your part. Why not? Are you thinking about Connor? I know you like him a lot. Otherwise, you wouldn't be over there so much. Are you like his girlfriend or something now?"

No question in her mind, she was blushing big time. "No, Joey, I'm just his friend," she said firmly. "Connor and I do not have a relationship in the way you mean." And they never would.

"He hasn't been around much lately. I miss him, you know?"

She knew. She nodded.

"He makes me feel…I don't know. He makes me feel like it's okay to do stupid things sometimes. He never laughs at me when I do. Instead he gets that serious kind of frown thing where his eyebrows grow together, like he's really studying what I'm saying, like anything I say is important. Like I could be somebody someday, you know?"

Again, she knew. "I know exactly," she said. "And you already are somebody."

Joey smiled. "That's what he would say, too. Wish he were here."

So did Alyssa. And she also wished something else. That she could ignore what Joey's words had made her realize. These children belonged to Connor, heart and soul. They loved him. They needed him.

She loved him, too, but she couldn't have him, not for more than a few hours of pleasure. The things she wanted were far removed from his own wants and needs.

When her trial period here was up, could she go on working for a man she loved and could never have?

Not without killing a part of herself. She'd come to help these children, she'd come to stay. But Connor was the Haven, and the children needed him for more than they needed her.

They needed him now, just as she did.

Come home, Connor. Quickly, she thought.

But once he was home, what then? What would she do when this last week of her month was up?

* * *

The place smelled like an office building. It felt like an office building. The sounds that surrounded him—shuffling of papers, heels clicking on tiled floors—were the kinds of sounds one associated with an office building, Connor thought as he waited to be shown in to see Jonathan Desworth.

There was absolutely nothing here to hint of espionage or criminal intent. Nothing a man could lay a finger on. He hadn't felt any instant psychic connection with a long-lost brother, his soul twin, so to speak.

Wild-goose chase, he thought, feeling somewhat foolish. But just then, a secretary came to lead him in to meet Desworth, and he clicked into gear. He'd sat in a hundred such offices. He was used to meeting with other inventors, and he knew the right questions to ask.

Think of it as simple research, not a life-changing, possibly world-saving event, he told himself. He tilted his head and thanked the young woman as he and Drifter followed her through the door into a carpeted room.

"Mr. Quinn," a man's voice said.

"Mr. Desworth." Connor held out his hand.

"I understand you're interested in the Redcom 7000. I'm pretty proud of that little puppy."

Connor raised his brows. "Little puppy" wasn't exactly how he'd describe something as complex as the invention they were discussing. Still, all inventors had their quirks. It was the business of working alone and praying for creativity twenty-four hours a day.

"You have reason to be proud. Let me ask you a few questions. Now that the 7000 is ready to expand its market, I'm sure there will be an interest in the history of such a simple yet amazingly complex system. Would you mind telling me how you came up with the idea?"

Desworth whistled. "It's pretty boring."

"Not to another inventor."

"Wouldn't you rather hear something about its features?"

"You could tell me about that, too," he said, although he already knew all the features intimately.

Desworth launched into a whirlwind explanation of what the 7000 could do. He talked fast, and his words were slick, like a salesman angling for the catch of the day.

"And what inspired you to invent something like this?" Connor asked.

"Well, there was a need. Necessity... Well, you know the saying."

"I know, but I'm more interested in the process. I like to think that what I'm investing in is unique, that there's a history behind it. I'm an inventor myself."

"They told me that." Desworth drummed his fingers on the table.

No problem, Connor thought. He'd met any number of inventors who were nervous when forced into public situations. But shouldn't there be some sense of connection between him and his brother? Damn, he admitted, he wanted there to be something, some feeling, something more than annoyance that the man couldn't even control his fingers. How could he work with such tiny sophisticated circuitry such as that which made up the 7000?

"So there were no 'Ah-hah!' moments like the one

Gilbert Dorban experienced when inventing the Dorban regulator?''

''The— No, I don't think there was anything like that, but it was a very satisfying moment when we finally had the breakthrough, I'll tell you that.''

''And what was the breakthrough?''

''Oh, I can't share that. Professional secret, you know.''

''I know how the 7000 works, Mr. Desworth. Shall I explain it?'' And without waiting for an answer, Connor dove in, detailing every part of the system. He understood it the way most people wouldn't, because he'd examined every inch before he'd agreed to install it and because of what he was. ''There's nothing about it that is a secret, even though it's an incredible device.''

To his credit, Desworth made an admirable attempt to talk shop after that and to sell Connor several other 7000s, which Connor went along with. No need to raise any more suspicions than he already had with his incredibly nosy questions. He wouldn't expect any inventor to share all his secrets. He certainly wouldn't share his.

Still, as Connor climbed back into his limo, he was aware of a great sense of letdown. There were two things he was sure of. Jonathan Desworth didn't have what it took to pull off something as complex as the WBH, and, if he was the inventor of the Redcom 7000, as all the literature suggested, then he was most definitely not the sole inventor.

Connor told the driver to take him back to the airport and wondered where he would go from here. He'd come away with more questions than answers.

And he had yet to locate his brother.

* * *

The plane ride home was uneventful, except for the fact that there were a greater number of children aboard than usual. The woman sitting next to him was talkative. She told him that she was six months pregnant.

"I can't wait," she said. "This is my second. I gave up a promising career to have babies, and I've never looked back. I've always wanted children. They're such a joy."

And she turned to catch hold of a child who was apparently dashing down the aisle.

"Stay in your seat, Dennie," she whispered. Her voice was filled with love.

That would be the way Alyssa would be when she became a mother. If necessary, she would give up her career and never look back. After seeing her in action and living with her nurturing, Connor could tell that she had been born to be a mother.

An ache spread within Connor. Dull at first, it became sharper and more intense as he listened to the mother whisper lovingly to her son. At one point he was sure she was talking to her unborn child as well.

"Life will be good," she was saying. "Wondrous, promising."

Connor breathed in one long, harsh breath. What if he had gotten Alyssa pregnant? He'd been careful, but still, those things could happen. Would she be sitting here months from now making those same promises to a child of his?

She'd want to. She surely would want to, but there was no way that a mother could promise the unborn child of Connor Quinn that life would be wondrous and promising. Her pregnancy would be fraught with worry, and who knew what kind of monstrosity would be the result of their union? A union that had been exquisitely sweet could result in something ugly with an uncertain future.

Don't touch her again, he told himself. Don't risk ruining her tomorrows.

Alyssa met Connor at the door of the Haven, and after his noisy and boisterous reunion with the children, she finally managed to get him alone in her office.

Her first instinct was to launch herself into his arms, to lift her face to be kissed, but he was still and quiet, and he had put his glasses on again, so she did none of the things that she wanted to.

"How did it go? Did you find out anything? Did you find him?" she asked instead. She knew he had already met with Jake, but she hadn't pumped Jake for information. She wanted all her news to come straight from Connor.

"I found out a few things," he told her. "I suppose one could say that this excursion was a bust, except I'm still not sure what Desworth was all about. He didn't ring true. He didn't seem to know what he was talking about. I'm going to have to take another look at this when I have a chance to figure things out. The one thing I do know is that he isn't one of…us."

She didn't even have to ask what he meant by us. He was talking about the Proteans—Jake and himself and his siblings.

Jake spoke of his siblings with endearment. Connor

could barely allude to his brothers and sisters. She knew what that meant. She'd heard the stories. Connor had not only been abandoned by his father, he'd been jilted by his bride. Because he was different.

Now he was even more different than he'd believed at first. He was drawing into himself more and more. She could see it. She could feel it.

"The only important thing is that you're safe," she said, blurting out what she could no longer hold inside. "Thank God you're safe."

Her words managed to elicit a small smile from him, but he shook his head. "It would have been difficult to be anything else. Jake had three guards on me. Or so he told me."

"Well, of course he did. You're important to him, you're his brother. He wouldn't have wanted to find you only to lose you again."

"He told you that, did he?"

"Not in so many words. When we talked after you left, he did say that he wanted a chance to get to know you."

He tilted his head. "You talked after I left?"

Alyssa squirmed on her chair, and Connor caught her hand.

"What did you talk about?"

She didn't answer at first.

"Alyssa?"

She blew out a breath. "All right, I can't lie. I called and asked him to make sure you didn't get killed."

"You didn't think I could take care of myself."

"No, it's not that. It's just that—"

"You might have been right. I do have limitations.

As I told you just a couple of days ago, I couldn't protect you and the children, even though I'd want to. If someone came at me with a gun, I'd be a dead man. So I guess I should thank you.''

But he didn't sound grateful. He sounded angry. At her or at himself, she wondered.

"I was worried," she said stiffly. "Is it a crime to want a person you care about to stay alive?"

"No, it's not," he said gently, taking her chin in his palm. "But some things are a crime. I thought about that while I was out there, the fact that I took risks with you. I want you to know that I enjoyed touching you. I more than enjoyed it, I reveled in feeling your skin beneath my hands. It was an experience like no other I've had before or will have in the future. But I should never have touched you. I'm not going to do it again. It was wrong, both morally and professionally. I'm your boss, and I gave you a trial period. To float sex into that mix was, indeed, a crime.''

"It wasn't just sex."

"No, but it was still wrong. You could have gotten pregnant."

"We took precautions."

"There are no precautions that are one hundred percent effective. I can't risk having children, Alyssa, especially not now. It wouldn't be fair to you."

"Don't I get to decide what's fair to me?"

He shook his head. "Not in this case. Not when I'm donating so much flawed genetic material. It has to be my choice, and I don't want children."

And she knew there was more. What he intended to follow that up with, but was too much of a gentleman to say, was, "And I don't want you." Oh, he cared for her, she was sure of that. He wasn't indifferent to her body or her person, but he didn't want a relationship, nothing that would involve risk or handing over his heart.

She could take that. It was ripping her apart, but she could take that because she had no right to ask him for more. But the children... He was a man made to have children. He already had children who adored him. He should have more.

She opened her mouth to tell him so, to protest, and, as if he anticipated her move, he held his hand up.

"I'm sorry I complicated your life." He took her hand in his own, brushing a kiss across her knuckles.

Such an innocent move, such a burning inside her.

Being touched by Connor would never be innocent or simple or meaningless. He saw things, and there were things she didn't want him to see. Like the state of her heart at this moment.

Alyssa jerked her hand away.

He took a visible breath, then stepped away from her. It felt like a final move, symbolic of the fact that he was ending something that had never truly had a chance to start.

"Are the children in bed already?" he asked.

She couldn't speak at first and he waited patiently. She wondered how many times in his life he had had to wait for someone to realize that shaking a head or nodding wasn't enough. And that was enough to send her struggling for her voice. "They wanted to wait up to say good-night to you. You could read them their story if you like."

"I'd like that," he said, and he moved off toward the wing of the Haven where the children slept.

She watched him go, this wonderful man and his dog. A tall, strong figure.

But alone. By choice, she reminded herself.

In a few days her trial period would be up.

She was in love with the man who was the heart of Woodland Haven, a man these children needed as they needed no other.

If she stayed, she would dry up of loneliness and hurt, and a man with Connor's heightened abilities would see that.

It would destroy him that he'd done that to her.

But still, he wouldn't budge, because he considered himself flawed. And he would not risk reproducing.

She was a risk to him. It was time for her to contact the board.

Fifteen

Connor had only been up a short while when the doorbell rang the next morning. He hoped that Mrs. Welsh was getting rid of whoever it was. He wasn't in the mood to be nice, and already felt like enough of an ogre after his meeting with Alyssa yesterday.

He'd hurt her, no doubt of that. He'd been cold and clinical and abrupt. Hadn't even bothered to tell her some things that were important. Like the fact that he appreciated all she'd done for the Haven, and the fact that she was the best thing that had happened to his kids in years.

As soon as he got rid of whoever was at the door, he was going to have to make sure Alyssa knew that he valued her as an employee and as a person. She'd brought life to the Haven, and damn it, he should have said so.

Instead he'd been too caught up in the pain of explaining to her, as well as to himself, why he couldn't have her when he wanted her so badly.

''Mr. Quinn,'' Mrs. Welsh said from the doorway.

''That's all right,'' a soft voice said. ''I'll see myself in unannounced, Mrs. Welsh. Thank you.''

Connor raised his head at her voice. ''Alyssa?''

Her footsteps brought her close.

"Why are you here?" he continued. "Is something wrong? Why didn't you call?"

She didn't answer right away. Then she moved closer still. "This isn't the kind of message a person should give another person over the phone."

Fear rushed through him in deep waves. "Is something wrong? Is someone hurt? Is it you? Joey?"

Alyssa placed her hand on his sleeve and he caught her fingers with his other hand. "You're nervous," he said. "Trembling."

She tugged at her hand, but he didn't let go. "Not exactly nervous, just...anticipating."

"Anticipating what?" She'd sounded far too light-hearted. Her voice didn't match what he felt when he touched her. Panic was surging through her, and yet she insisted that she wasn't panicked.

"I've decided that your reputation for knowing things that other people only guess at is well deserved. That first day that we met—"

"I behaved shabbily."

"You behaved as anyone in your position should have," she said indignantly. "Furthermore, you were right about me."

Tension climbed though his body. "In what way?"

"In the way that you indicated that I wasn't really the right person for this job."

"You're perfect for this job. I think I told you some time ago that the trial period was over almost before it began. Who better to run the Haven?"

"I don't know. Someone, though. Not me."

"Alyssa?" He fought the urge to pull her into his arms and ask her to take back her last words.

"No, you were right. I...I wouldn't fit in here for long. I'm a rather ambitious woman. I have places I need to go and other projects I need to pursue. Now that things are running smoothly at the Haven, I've discovered that I'm willing to turn the orphanage over to someone else to maintain."

"Someone else?" His voice came out in a regrettable roar.

"I've already given Evelyn Wentworth my resignation. I've promised the board that I'll make sure there are competent people in here for the children, and I'm already going through my records searching for someone who would truly be a credit to the Haven."

"You're a credit to the Haven."

She placed her other hand over his then. "Connor, we both know that this won't work. You were right. We shouldn't have gotten involved, but since we did, I have to go. It's just too difficult. We can't go back to what we were and pretend that nothing ever happened. It did happen, and I'm not sorry that it did. But you were correct that nothing can come of it, so I'm going. I'm dealing with this in the only way I know how, but I promise you I won't fail the children and the Haven. I'll do my best to make sure they don't feel abandoned."

Don't go, he wanted to demand.

But of course she would go. She had to. He hadn't given her any choice. He had no choices to offer her.

If he did, he would give her anything, everything, all of himself, all he had, and he would never look back.

But that wasn't the way it was.

"When are you going?" he asked tersely.

"Today. I've already made arrangements for a temporary director to come in. She's very good, the best. I promise you that."

"You're deserting them."

"Don't say that."

"That's how they'll see it."

"No, they're smarter than that. They'll know that I love them. I'll make them know, and I'll stay in touch."

"Will you? For how long?"

She swallowed. "As long as they want me to. Children are a lifetime commitment."

"Yes, they are."

In a sudden switch, she turned her hand quickly and caught his between both of her palms. "You should have some. You're perfect father material, Connor. Don't deny that you love them."

"I would never deny that."

But he would deny other things. This was clearly painful for her. He could make it easier. He could give her his blessings. He could stop trying to hold her here.

He lifted her hands to his face. "I love them, Alyssa, but I can't have my own. Don't even suggest it."

She didn't. Instead, she sighed sadly as she rose on her toes and kissed him. She wound her arms around him and nearly stole what was left of his heart after it had shattered when she had told him she was leaving.

He couldn't help himself then. He kissed her back, slowly, fully. He gave and gave and took and took.

"Be happy," he said as he let her go.

He listened for her response, but all he heard was the echoing of her footsteps as she walked out of his life for the last time.

* * *

"Will you come and see us, Alyssa?" Letice begged as Alyssa said her goodbyes. "Do you really have to go?"

"Yes, I'm afraid I do, sweetheart," she said. "Sometimes things have to end before we want them to. I'd like to stay here with you, but there are circumstances that prevent me from doing that."

"You're in love with Connor, aren't you?" Kanika's voice rang pure and true.

Honesty was important, Alyssa told herself, but she couldn't be totally honest here. "There are all kinds of love," she said. "So yes, I guess I do love Connor, but it's not the marrying and settling-down kind. It isn't the build-a-family kind."

"He listens for you," Letice said. "When he's here, his expression changes when you come into the room, and when you talk, he smiles. Most of the time."

Alyssa almost managed to smile at that comment. Letice wasn't telling any secrets. Alyssa knew Connor felt something special for her. Not what she felt for him, which was so overpowering that she was shredding into little pieces at the thought of leaving him, but still he felt something beyond lust and more than just friendship. But none of that meant anything. If she stayed, they would just torture each other.

"Don't go, Alyssa," Joey said, and Alyssa wondered if she could work out any way to stay. Joey needed so much. He didn't need another person skipping off just after he'd started to trust.

She dropped to her knees beside him. "I will never leave you," she said fiercely. "Never. You'll get so many e-mails that the mailbox here will be clogged. I'll send so many cards and letters that it will take you hours to read them. And I'll call you. All the time. And you'll call me, too. Whenever you need me, you call. I don't care if it's three in the morning. If you have a nightmare and you need someone to talk to, you wake me up. I won't mind a bit. Because I love you, you know. I love all of you so very much." And she threw her arms around him and hugged his little body tight.

Tears were streaming down her face.

"Why are you leaving us if it makes you so sad, Alyssa?" Bud asked, kicking at the rug so hard that Alyssa just knew Connor was going to have to get it repaired.

She couldn't tell them why, because if she told the truth, they would hate Connor. They would hold it against him, and Connor loved them beyond belief. Moreover, he was the heart of this place. He gave it more than money; he gave it life. And it gave him the only love he would allow himself to take.

"I'm going because there are things I need to do in another place," she said, thinking of the truths she could actually tell. "Somewhere there's a boy that doesn't have a man like Connor, a boy who needs someone to teach him that he matters a whole lot."

"Why don't you just bring him here?" Petra asked. "We'd love him."

And despite her best intentions, Alyssa's face crumpled. "I know you would, sweetie. You all would do that. But sometimes little boys can't leave their homes. They need the adults to come to them, to help them, to save them. Right now you're all safe. Look what a great home Connor has made for you, and look how much you're loved by not only Connor, but Mrs. Jones and Mrs. Morrissey and every teacher here. They all love you very much. So, you let them know that you love them, too, and send me lots of news. I do have to go, but I'm going to miss you horribly.''

And soon she had hugged every child, she had said every last goodbye, she had watched Nola Morrissey wipe tears away with her apron, and then she was walking out the door, the Haven at her back.

On the way out of town, she couldn't help herself; she drove past his house and sat there for a minute in the dark, wondering what he was doing inside. And then with tears streaming down her face, so many she could barely see to drive safely, she fled in the dark.

There was no haven for her here anymore.

Connor got up from his keyboard and wandered the room. It was pointless to pretend that he was working. He'd been trying to lie to himself all day, but the fact remained that he had absolutely no interest in work or in anything else, either.

She'd gone. He'd let her go, making no real attempt to stop her.

And it was probably for the best for her. But for him it was pure torture.

''So what was I supposed to do?'' he muttered. ''Pretend I could be what she needed? She needs life, marriage, children. I can't give her children, and there are so many men who can. Men who will love and cherish her and be all that she needs.''

He'd done the right thing. He knew he had, but…

Connor slammed his fist into the wall just as the phone rang.

"Hello," he said, ignoring the sting in his hand as he grasped the receiver. It might be Alyssa. She'd promised to check up on the children. Of course, Mrs. Morrissey or Edwina would be the logical people to call in such a case. Connor held his breath.

"Connor, what are you doing with yourself?" Jake's voice came over the line.

"I'm not ignoring my mission for you, if that's what you mean. I'm still checking other avenues, hoping to find Gideon."

"That's not what I meant. I know you're still looking for Gideon, but what are you doing about you? I just talked to someone at the Haven. They told me that you'd let Alyssa go."

"She wanted to go."

"You're sure about that?"

No, he wasn't sure about that at all. He'd known that leaving had been painful for her, but apparently staying had been more painful.

Connor sighed. "Drop it, Jake. Don't interfere in things you know nothing of."

"You're my brother, Connor."

"Yes, but I'm not used to being a member of a family."

"Then we should remedy that. As soon as possible. I have a feeling that a good dose of company is just what you need right now. It's time, Connor."

"I'm not good company right now, Jake."

"Because you've just made a big mistake and let the woman you love slip away."

"Because I've just done the right thing, but it was still something that wasn't easy."

"All right, have it your way, but don't push your family aside because you don't think you'd be good company. There's a bond between us, Connor, one unlike any other brothers and sisters could ever share. We need you to complete the circle, and I'm vain enough to think that you might benefit from spending some time with us, as well. At any rate, I'm getting all kinds of pressure from the clan. They want to at least get the chance to meet you, Connor. You're a part of us. Say yes."

He wanted to hide and lick his wounds.

"We've all gone through hell, Connor, and come through it. Every one of us has missing parts of his life. Don't be another missing part. Gretchen's pregnant. She doesn't need more things to worry about."

"You play dirty, brother."

"I know. It's just part of the reason why I've been put on the case involving the WBH. Sometimes more than genius is needed."

Sometimes that feeling that vibrated between people of like minds and talents was needed, Connor thought, remembering again how he'd doubted that Jonathan Desworth could really be the inventor of the Redcom 7000.

"Gretchen...our sister...is she really worried? Would that affect her baby?"

"She wants to meet you, Connor. Badly. So do Marcus and Faith, who's also pregnant. Why not give them a chance? We can have you back in no time."

"I'll think about it."

''Think about it now.''

He did. Jake was right. He'd put off meeting his siblings because he didn't know how to be a part of something, most especially a family. But Jane, his former director at the Haven and the closest thing to a mother he'd had, would have urged him to go, to mingle. She'd always said that he needed to climb outside himself now and then.

And if he left, he wouldn't have time to think about Alyssa. There would be no temptation to check up on her, and he would be forced to leave her alone.

That more than anything helped him make the decision.

In only a matter of hours, he and Drifter were on an airplane.

Alyssa sat in her cramped little apartment outside of Chicago and scrolled through the e-mail messages from the children. Thank goodness she hadn't given up her place when she left for Boston.

''We love you. Please come visit us soon,'' said one from Kanika.

''I even miss your spinach surprise,'' another one read, this time from Letice.

''If you come back to visit us soon, I promise I'll show you how to throw a football, and not like a girl, either,'' Bud promised.

There were more, as well. The messages were all kid-sweet, offering promises and love and acceptance. Not a word of retribution among them, even though Alyssa had kicked herself plenty of times in the two days since she'd been gone. Even though she was backpedaling like crazy, missing them all, hating herself for hurting them, thinking that she'd never hurt this badly in a lifetime filled with hurts.

And worse, there had been no messages from Joey.

Not one, even though she'd sent him many.

He was protecting himself, building armor. She was sure of it.

And not a single message from any of the children had carried any information about Connor. It was driving her crazy, making her insane with worry.

Joey, her little boy who had been abandoned and hurt so many times.

Connor, who had also been abandoned and no longer allowed anyone inside the closed doors to his heart.

Connor was a loner. She'd known that going in, and still she'd allowed herself to love him. She couldn't not love him, and now that she was too far away to know what was going on, she couldn't stop worrying.

Was he still out there looking for Gideon?

Was Gideon aware of that? Was Jake making sure that Connor was safe?

Were Joey and Connor taking care of each other? Had they already put her out of their minds?

It would be best for them if they had.

But she would not be able to let go so easily herself.

Maybe she should call Jake and just check up on them. He would know what was going on. It couldn't hurt, could it? Just this once?

But when she tried to get in touch with Jake, she had to leave a message. And he didn't return her call.

Sixteen

Connor sat in the midst of his brothers and sisters in the warmth of the sun on the island of Brunhia and listened to them all talking at once. It wasn't much different from being at the Haven, he mused, shaking his head as he smiled slowly.

"What?" Marcus asked gruffly.

"Nothing. It's just that I've never been part of a family gathering before. It's going to take some getting used to."

"I know what you mean," Faith said. "Or maybe I don't exactly. Our memories were suppressed. You never really had any. At least not of us. I hate that. I'm sure Violet is up in heaven scolding Henry right now. It would have broken her heart if she'd known that he'd hidden you away and let her think you were dead. As it was, it broke her heart, anyway."

"Yes, to lose a child…" Gretchen reached out and barely touched Connor's hand. "May I?" she asked.

In answer, he turned his hand over and took hers in his own. "Do you worry about the baby?" he asked.

"I'm an expectant mom. That means I worry. Right, Faith? Samantha?"

"Every day," Samantha, Marcus's wife, who was also pregnant, agreed.

"Carrying a baby, wonderful as it is, can be unnerving," Faith said. "I still can't believe that a child is growing inside me. I feel as if I've been given a gift, but sometimes I'm afraid I'll wake up and it won't be real. I imagine most expectant moms feel that way."

Connor managed a small smile. "I suppose that's true, but I wasn't talking about the usual things that pregnant women worry about. I mean do any of you worry because…of what we are."

"What are we?" Marcus asked.

"Different," Connor answered.

"But different in a good way," Faith's husband, Luke, said. "The best way."

"Forgive me, but that sounds like love talking," Connor said.

Faith laughed. "Thank you, big brother. I do believe you've offered me my first insult. At least my first from you."

He scrubbed an impatient hand back through his hair and cleared his throat. "Jake, help me out here, will you? You know what I'm talking about."

"Haven't a clue," Jake said, but there was amusement in his voice.

"Sounds like someone's got hold of you and been telling you lies," Gretchen said. "Or maybe it's understandable. Our father took you and—"

"I believe the word is *dumped*, Gretchen," Marcus said. "Henry tossed Connor, here, aside. Not right," he said. "But Gretchen's on to something. That would give you a different view of things. The rest of us were never taught to be ashamed of our differences. You shouldn't be, either. You're unique."

"And my baby will be unique," Gretchen said. "Think about it, Connor. It's no different from being an extremely talented pianist or a gifted physician."

"Except someone fooled around with the DNA to make us that way," Connor answered. "We don't know how that will play out down the road. It's a gamble."

"Everything's a gamble," Faith said softly. "Don't hide yourself from life or from us, big brother, just because our father was foolish enough not to see your value. We see it. We want to get to know you. I do. And if you didn't have that altered DNA, you wouldn't be you, would you?" She moved close and placed a hand on his shoulder.

"Hell, man, you're a genius. What's so wrong with that?" Marcus asked. "I'm proud to know that you're my brother, and from what I've heard there are any number of women who wouldn't object to sharing some of your DNA."

Connor sucked in a breath. "Jake, what have you been telling them?"

"Me?" Jake asked, with exaggerated innocence in his voice. "I've only told them the truth. We certainly didn't discuss your love life."

"You think I can't do my own research?" Marcus asked. "You think we've all been sitting here twiddling our fingers while Jake tried to smooth talk you into coming around to meet the family? We already know all there is to know about you, and we like what we know."

"And as for my baby, Connor," Gretchen said softly. "My baby will be what it will be, and I'll love him or her no matter what goes right or what goes wrong. I'll love my child the way any mother would. Unconditionally. There's nothing that could change that.''

"Life could be hard if the baby's born…different.''

"Then Kurt and I will do our best to make sure that our child has all the love and all the skills to deal with that.''

"And our babies will have lots of loving aunts and uncles to help out, too,'' Faith said. "Because we all know what it is to be different, and it's our very differences that have brought us to where we are. They're what brought you here, too.''

"And it's those differences that have matched us with mates who love us for what we are. We're all happily settled,'' Gretchen said.

"All except Jake and you,'' Marcus said, his voice troubled. "We need to find a woman for you, Jake. You too, Connor.''

Suddenly Jake moved closer to Connor as if the two of them could fend off the matchmaking plans of their brother.

"Thanks, but I'll pass,'' Jake said. "You know what happened between Tara and me.''

"She was just wrong for you,'' Gretchen said.

"Maybe.'' Jake didn't sound convinced.

"You haven't met the right woman, either, have you, Connor?'' Faith asked, and there was something hesitant in her voice. He remembered that Marcus had said they knew all there was to know about him. No doubt they knew about Alyssa.

He remembered Gretchen's fierce speech about her baby and how she would love it no matter what. He knew that Alyssa would feel that way, too. Did that make it right for him to approach her, knowing that loving a child who was different would create difficulties and hard times. A woman in such circumstances would need special skills.

Just like loving some of the children at the Haven had required special skills.

Which his Alyssa seemed to have in abundance.

"Does a man have a right to ask a woman to face the fire with him, not knowing what the outcome will be?" he asked softly, ignoring Faith's question.

It was Gretchen who answered. "Does he have the right to withhold love from her because he isn't sure she's capable of standing up to the challenges loving him might bring?"

"That's not the problem. She's capable," he said, realizing just how much that was true. Alyssa had made him feel more whole than he had ever felt in his life. "She's more than capable," he amended. "She's... amazing."

He could have sworn he heard hands slapping, and a low chuckle from Jake. "Leave it to Gretchen to lay it on the line," Jake said. "So what are you waiting for, brother of mine?"

"I'm not sure I have a right to ask her for anything. I think I may have hurt her." Connor's throat closed up at the thought of how hard Alyssa had fought to earn a place at the Haven, of how freely she'd loved the children and how she'd left.

Because he'd made it impossible for her to stay.

"I didn't give her any choice other than leaving," he told his siblings. "What kind of jerk would do that and then turn around and ask a woman to come back?"

"A man so much in love he's acting crazy," Marcus said. "Believe me, I understand, so just go to her. Ask her. Do whatever you have to do. If she says no, we'll come beg her to take you, and that's a promise. Now that we've found a new brother, we want him to be happy."

Connor shook his head, but he managed to smile. "Thanks, but this is definitely something I want to do myself."

"Then go. Don't wait," Gretchen said. "Tell her how you feel."

He could at least do that. He could apologize and give her a choice for once. If he found out she was suffering, he would insist that she return to the Haven. He'd leave home and all that he loved before he'd hurt her again.

"Yes, tell her how you feel," Faith said. "Send her our love and tell her we've been dying to meet her ever since Jake told us about the two of you."

"Jake?" he asked, crossing his arms.

"Hey, don't look at me that way. I only said that I thought you had met a woman who was a match for you."

She *was* a match for him. He wanted her to be his for all time, but he'd spent every day he'd known her telling her that he wasn't interested in settling down.

She liked him well enough. She'd been willing to come to his bed, but did she feel more? Had he hurt her too much for her to ever trust him? Or was she already looking for another kind of man, one who was smart enough to woo her from the start. One who would promise her babies and love and her heart's desire.

When he had never promised her a thing.

* * *

Alyssa tried to work on her résumé. She'd been trying to work on it for days, but whenever she sat down to concentrate, all she saw was Connor.

"Idiot," she told herself. "Forget him. He didn't want you." But she knew it was more than that. Connor had wanted her in some ways, but not in the ways that counted the most.

So get over it, she told herself. Move on.

She was trying to, but that thing he did, that awareness of her when he touched her—she was beginning to think that it worked both ways. Because she knew him in ways she had never known another man, she loved him in ways she'd never loved, and forgetting him was completely impossible. She would move on, but she would never forget.

A knocking at her door broke into her thoughts. Impatiently she let out a small muffled cry of frustration. She couldn't deal with company now.

"Who is it?" she asked, peering through the peephole on the door. But before he'd even had time to answer, she pulled the door open, letting in a full view of the man she loved and had never thought to see again.

"Connor," she said, hoping her voice was cool. "What…what are you doing here?"

"Inviting myself in," he said, moving forward into her house and her space and almost edging up against her body.

Her heart pounded furiously, and she hoped he couldn't tell. She took a step back, knowing that if she got too close she would ignore all good sense and touch him. It had been so hard to leave him.

"I'm sure you have a reason," she said. "Is something wrong with the children? Are you having trouble finding a replacement for me?"

"The children were fine when I saw them yesterday," he said, ignoring her attempt to step away as he drew closer still. "And I haven't even started looking for a replacement for you."

"Why?" She moved back two feet.

"How are you?" he asked, ignoring her question. He closed the door behind him. He took Drifter's harness off and instructed him to sit. Then he closed the gap between Alyssa and himself again. "The children tell me that you've kept in touch. And that you haven't even asked about me." He reached out and touched her cheek.

Warmth flooded her; longing rushed through her. She struggled to control her breathing, to keep her body from responding to his touch. He would know how deep her feelings ran if she did. He probably already knew, so she schooled her mind to think of other things. Boring things. She tried to pretend that his touch meant nothing to her. And when she knew that pretending was useless, she scooted back yet again. Now she was up against the desk that took up most of the space in her tiny living room.

"I'm making you nervous," he said softly.

"No," she protested, too strongly. "Yes," she admitted, sure that he'd already discerned her lie. "I didn't think I'd ever see you again. I can't imagine why you've come."

He stroked his finger down her cheek. "You left in such a hurry, before the trial period was completely over, that I was caught off guard. Now I've had a chance to rethink things, and I've decided that we have some business to finish."

Wordlessly she shook her head, his finger sliding against her skin.

"Yes," he whispered. "Tell me why you really left. I know it wasn't a career thing. You love those kids too much."

"I—"

"Make it good," he ordered. "Make it the truth. You've never dodged an issue before."

"All right, then. It was you."

"You didn't like me."

"You know that's not true, but I knew there was no way— You warned me away, froze me out."

He framed her face with his hands. "I promise not to do that again. I'll keep things warm."

She placed her hands over his, knowing that touching him in any way was a big mistake but helpless to stop herself. "Connor, please stop. You're hurting me."

Immediately he let her go, even though both of them knew that she didn't mean that he was physically hurting her.

He turned from her and blew out a breath. "You're right. As it is, I've already taken advantage of you. Too many times."

"You know it's not that. Anything I gave you, I gave freely."

"But you said I hurt you. Tell me how. Tell me all of it."

His voice was so sad that Alyssa's throat ached, and she moved to stand close behind him. Still, she couldn't answer. To do so would be to spill her heart and leave herself defenseless.

"I know I'm a difficult man," Connor began, and she couldn't help but shake her head, her hair brushing his skin.

"You don't agree?"

"Not really. I suppose you can be a difficult man sometimes, when you feel there's a danger of injustice being done, but that wouldn't be the first thing I'd note about you."

"No?" And he turned to her and placed his hands on her shoulders. "So, what do you see when you look at me?"

Alyssa sighed. She knew what he thought others saw, and what his former fiancée had seen. His blindness.

That was so wrong. So, dangerous though it might be, she had to clear up a few things and tell him the truth.

She cleared her throat and gazed up at that gorgeous face. She felt his body close to hers and shivered slightly with need. "When I look at you, I see a genius, a stubbornly independent man, a kind man."

"Kind?" he asked, his voice rough, his breath warm on her face.

She knew he didn't think himself kind at all, and at first she couldn't begin to find the words to tell him how many small acts of kindness she'd witnessed in him. The very fact that he was so big and yet so gentle with her...

"Alyssa, *have* I hurt you?" he asked, and she felt the tension and fear residing within him.

"Never intentionally," she answered truthfully.

"But I have."

"You couldn't help it."

"Damn it, Alyssa, that's a lie if ever I heard one. A man is responsible for his actions. I knew I shouldn't have touched you, but I did, anyway, and I knew—"

The agony in his voice was evident. She couldn't have that, and quickly she slipped her fingertips over his lips.

"It was me. I was the one responsible for any hurt I felt. I just couldn't seem to help it. I—"

And then his arms were around her, pulling her close. "What I can't help is loving you," he said fiercely. "Even though I know it's wrong."

His voice was anguished, but joy was coursing through Alyssa. "Why is it wrong?"

"I'm afraid I'll fail you, be unable to be all you need and give you all you need."

"And what do I need?"

"Babies, for one thing. Healthy, normal babies." He started to pull away, but this time she was the one who stalked him, stepping close when he would have backed away. She placed a hand on his chest and rose on her toes so that she could bring her lips close to his. "Connor, don't make my decisions for me. If you and I were to have a baby, that would be wonderful, but if we didn't, that would be all right, too."

"And if we did, we don't know what that child might turn out like," he said, his body tense and unyielding.

"You're wrong. *I* know."

"What do you know?"

"I know that any child you and I made together would be special. Very special."

"And you'd be all right if there were no babies?" He relaxed slightly and his arms slipped down around her, locking behind her waist. She rested against his chest.

"If all I ever did was stand here in your arms, I'd be happy," she said.

He laughed, and the sound rumbled through her. "I definitely want more of you than this," he told her.

She tipped her head back and kissed him quickly, her lips soft against his. "I want you, too. All of you."

"You make me feel I'm a part of the world rather than separate from it," he said, holding her close as he nuzzled her lips.

The words were a bit stilted, and Alyssa knew that such admissions didn't come easily for him. "You've always been a part of the world," she said. "A truly special part. You're the finest man I know."

He groaned as her lips touched him just beneath his jaw. "Do you have any inkling how much I love you?" he asked her.

"You never told me," she said, reproachfully.

"I was afraid I'd ruin your life. I'm still not sure I won't."

"You couldn't. Only being without you could do that. You *are* going to ask me to come back, aren't you?" And she couldn't keep the uncertainty from her voice.

"I'm going to beg you to come back," he said, dropping to one knee. "And then I'm going to do everything I can to convince you to marry me."

She slid to the ground and wrapped her arms around his neck. "Yes, I'll marry you. Does this mean our trial period is finally over?"

Connor laughed. "Alyssa, my love, I have a confession to make. I know I've hinted before that you won me over quickly, but I don't think I've explained just how quickly. Your trial period was over before you walked out of the room that very first day. In my heart I already knew that I'd met someone who was going to turn my world upside down."

"Upside down is good?"

"It's excellent," he confessed, sitting back and gathering her onto his lap. "With you, it's all good and right. At last."

She moved against him, cuddling close. "I wasn't sure we had a future."

"Might be tough," he confessed. "I'm going to keep looking for Gideon. That might be dangerous. You all right with that?"

She turned her head and kissed his jaw. "You have to. I'll help you in whatever way I can."

"And I was thinking of moving in with the children. Even if you and I never have children of our own, we'll love the ones we already have."

"I can't wait to tell them. I'm worried about Joey."

"I stopped by to get their blessings before I came. I warned them that I might not be successful, so they're waiting to see if you agreed to have me. I probably shouldn't have said anything to them, got their hopes up, but I was nervous and acting stupid."

She turned in his arms then and looked up at him. "I love that you were nervous, you, who could have any woman on the planet."

"You know that's not true."

"Well then, those other women are just idiots."

He chuckled. "Keep thinking that way. Will you mind moving in with the kids?"

"I wouldn't have it any other way."

He nodded. "There's a plot of land in the country not far from here. I bought it some time ago, but yesterday when I knew I was coming for you, I started thinking that it would be a good vacation spot. The children could have a change of pace now and then. Would you like to go there to see it with me?"

"I would love to go anywhere with you. I'm going to love sharing and loving our children."

"Then we'll go," he said, lowering her to the carpeting. "In just a while, we'll go."

Alyssa's arms crept up around Connor's neck. "In just a while," she agreed as she touched her lips to his.

Connor sent Jerry back to Boston, and Alyssa and Connor called the children and told them they were getting married and moving to the Haven amidst whoops of excitement on the other end of the line.

"We'll be a family," Joey said.

"We'll be the best family ever," Alyssa promised as she and Connor turned the speakerphone on and told each and every child how much they loved them.

An hour later they were in the car as Alyssa drove up the road to the country lot that Connor had bought.

"Describe it to me," he said. "I want to see it through your eyes."

"It's beautiful," she said. "A big, rambling white and green farmhouse surrounded by lots of trees with a lake in the distance."

"I'm told the house isn't that big," he said. "I'll build more living space."

"It's perfect," she told him. "Especially because it's snowing." She stopped the car in the drive.

He gathered her to him and kissed her cold lips. "I hope it snows a lot," he whispered. "I remember a particularly wonderful snowy night."

"Umm, me, too. And it looks like it's going to snow a lot. Did you remember to tell Mrs. Welsh where we were going?"

"Yes. I called my sisters and brothers, too, since they were all sitting by the phone waiting to hear if you were foolish enough to take me on."

"They didn't say that," she said, hitting him lightly.

"No, they didn't. They said they knew they'd love you as much as they love me."

"That's nice."

He opened his door, let Drifter out, and the two of them circled the car so that Connor could open Alyssa's door. Suddenly he scooped her into his arms.

"Drifter can handle both of us?" she asked.

"Umm, he's a talented dog."

"Yes, he is. With a talented man to work for."

He put her down gently. "You make me more than I ever was before."

"No, you were always more than any man I'd ever known."

"Thanks to dear old dad and his experiments."

She placed her hands against his chest. "No, that's not it at all. It's more. Can I ask you a favor?"

"Ask and it's yours." He swooped in close and kissed her lips.

She smiled against his mouth. "All right," she whispered, pulling back slightly. "Describe me."

"Excuse me?"

She poked him in the chest. "You heard me. Describe me."

He chuckled as she poked him again. "Bossy, aren't you?"

She folded her arms, creating a barrier between their bodies. "It's my nature."

"Maybe, princess, but only partly. Because my description of you would include your honesty, your strength, your determination. You're a caring woman, and I love you for it."

"That's so nice," she said, her voice breaking as she kissed him. "See?"

He didn't see. "I only see you."

"Don't you realize that you see me in ways no one sees me?" she asked him. "You didn't once mention that I had a pretty face."

"I would if I could. I wish I could say that." He held her close against him in a fierce hug, but she shook her head.

"You don't need to. It doesn't matter. You see what's important, the only man ever to do that for me. And I see what's important in you. Connor, I don't care about how you were conceived or the mechanics of your birth or even your genetic makeup. I only care that you are who you are, and who you are is wonderful. You're the only man for me.''

He kissed her then, slowly, deeply and with passion. She cried out and pressed against him.

''Let's go inside now,'' she whispered.

In answer, he swung her into his arms again. ''I've had the house stocked with supplies. Enough so that we won't have to face the world for several days,'' he said, as she leaned and opened the door and he brought her into the warmth and slid her down his body. He released Drifter, who lay down by the hearth, and then Connor reached for Alyssa.

''That's good,'' she said, and she slid his coat from his body and clenched her fingers in the flannel of his shirt as she rose on her toes to kiss him. ''Because I have a lot of love I want to show you.''

''Show me,'' he whispered as he gathered her into his arms.

''Is there a trial period?'' she teased.

''Absolutely, my love. It's going to last the rest of our lives.'' And he tumbled her down on the nearest couch.

* * * * *

There are more secrets to reveal—
don't miss out!
Coming in March 2004 to
Silhouette Books

Widower Harrison Parker needed a nanny
for his three young children so he could
work on a top-secret government project.
But he hadn't counted on finding such a
beautiful and intriguing woman, who just
might capture his heart...

THE PARKER PROJECT
By
Joan Elliott Pickart

FAMILY SECRETS: *Five extraordinary*
siblings. One dangerous past.
Unlimited potential.

And now, for a sneak peak,
just turn the page...

One

Harrison got to his feet and went to the hearth, staring into the flames for a long moment before turning to look at Maggie again.

"Why?" he said quietly. "Why do I upset you?"

"It's just a combination of things," Maggie said, averting her eyes from Harrison's intense gaze. "My parents were older, we lived a very quiet, sedate life. I was shy, didn't have many friends, never dated in high school. The one relationship I had years ago with a man ended in disaster and I just feel safer alone, on my own. I'm quite contented with my life as it is. I'm just…just not comfortable around men, adults in general, as a matter of fact. It's nothing personal, Harrison."

"I see," he said slowly. "It seems to me that you have something that needs work, just as I do in my role of father, and this is a perfect opportunity for you to get started."

Maggie's head snapped up and she looked at Harrison.

"What do you mean?" she said, frowning.

"You need to move past your fear—or whatever you want to call it—of adults, of men in particular. I'm here. I'm a man. You can practice with me because I'm no threat to you. You've heard me say that I am not husband material, which means I'll never again become involved in a serious relationship on any level. I might date later, casual outings, but that's it.

"Therefore, you are perfectly safe with me. You can learn to relax, chat, interact with me and know I won't take advantage of you, nor ask anything of you. Get it?"

"I think that's borderline crazy, Harrison."

"No, it's not. You're teaching me how to be a father. I'll teach you how to enjoy the company of men. Sounds like a fair trade to me."

"Definitely crazy," Maggie said, getting to her feet. "I've got to go home."

"Whoa," Harrison said, closing the distance between them. "We came in here in the first place to discuss something about tomorrow. Remember?"

"Oh. Yes," Maggie said, then cleared her throat. "I thought maybe we could go get a Christmas tree with the kids right after school, then put it up and decorate it. It was just a thought. That is, if you even use a real tree."

"Sounds good, and yes, I like the smell of a real tree in the house, not an artificial one. I think that's a great idea. We'll start getting ready for the holiday season. This first one without Lisa is going to be very difficult for the kids, I imagine, so we might as well get it going and deal with the fallout."

"Yes, that's what I was thinking, too." Maggie paused. "Harrison, would you please back up a step or two? You're in my space, invading my comfort zone."

Harrison glanced down at the floor, mentally measuring the distance between them, then frowned as he looked at Maggie again.

"Your zone is oversized," he said.

"Well, that's for me to say. It *is* my zone, you know."

"I realize that," Harrison said, nodding, "but you're learning how to be comfortable around men, around me, remember?"

"I never agreed to your plan to—"

"Check this out, Maggie," Harrison interrupted. "If I was a man who was chatting with you and who also wished to kiss you—" he placed his hands lightly on her shoulders "—I'd need to be this close to you. If I backed up out of *your* comfort zone, I'd have to raise my voice to talk to you and the kiss would be impossible from that distance."

"I—"

"But if I'm here, in what is really quite a normal comfort zone for the average person," Harrison went on, "we can converse in normal tones and—" he lowered his head and brushed his lips over Maggie's "—things could progress further if they were meant to be."

Oh, dear heaven, Maggie thought. Harrison's lips fluttering over hers had been as light as a butterfly's wings. But she could still feel his lips, the lingering faint taste of him, and...

His hands. They were there on her shoulders, and the heat from them was suffusing her entire body. This was not a comfort zone, this was an erogenous zone, and it was...wonderful. Absolutely marvelous and— No, darn it, it was terrifying and she wanted no part of this. Then again…

"Maggie?" Harrison said, not removing his hands from her shoulders. "Do you still want me to back up, get out of your zone?"

"No. Yes. I don't know. You're confusing me, Harrison."

"That's good," he said. "If you're confused, then it means that your beliefs aren't etched in stone and can't be budged. There's no reason in the world for you to sentence yourself to a life alone, Maggie Conrad. Me? After the kids are grown and gone, then yeah, I'll be alone, and nothing can change that. But that's not true for you. It just isn't."

"You don't know me well enough to make such a statement, Harrison," Maggie said firmly.

"Don't I?"

Harrison moved his hands to frame Maggie's face, then lowered his head and captured her lips in a searing kiss. Maggie's hands flew up to splay on his chest with every intention of shoving him away, but the instant her palms felt the hard wall of muscle, she gripped handfuls of his sweater and pulled him closer.

Harrison parted Maggie's lips and delved into the dark sweetness beyond, savoring the taste of her, drinking of it like a thirsty man.

A little whimper caught in Maggie's throat.

A groan rumbled in Harrison's chest.

He broke the kiss, slowly, reluctantly, then dropped his hands from Maggie's flushed cheeks and took a step backward.

"You," he said, then cleared his throat when he

heard the gritty quality of his voice. "You are not meant to spend your life alone, magical Maggie. You are a very passionate, very desirable woman. I envy the man you fall in love with. He'd damn well better deserve who and what you are."

"Don't swear in the house," Maggie said, then drew a wobbly breath. "I have to go home. Now."

Harrison nodded. "Good night, Maggie."

She hurried across the room, grabbed her tote bag and coat and left the house before putting her coat on. Harrison shoved his hands into his pockets and stared at the door that had closed behind Maggie.

"Oh, yeah," he said, "I envy the man you fall in love with, Maggie. I truly do."

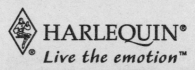

Silhouette®
Where love comes alive™

Five extraordinary siblings.
One dangerous past.
Unlimited potential.

Collect four (4) original proofs of purchase from the back pages of four (4) Family Secrets titles and receive a specialty themed free gift valued at over $20.00 U.S.!

Just complete the order form and send it, along with four (4) proofs of purchase from four (4) different Family Secrets titles to: Family Secrets, P.O. Box 9047, Buffalo, NY 14269-9047, or P.O. Box 613, Fort Erie, Ontario L2A 5X3.

Name (PLEASE PRINT)

Address   Apt. #

City   State/Prov.   Zip/Postal Code

Please specify which themed gift package(s)
you would like to receive:

❏ PASSION DT5N
❏ HOME AND FAMILY DT5P
❏ TENDER AND LIGHTHEARTED DT5Q

❏ Have you enclosed your proofs of purchase?

One Proof
Of Purchase
FSPOP9R

Remember—for each package selected, you must send four (4) original proofs of purchase. To receive all three (3) gifts, just send in twelve (12) proofs of purchase, one from each of the 12 Family Secrets titles.

Please allow 4-6 weeks for delivery. Shipping and handling included. Offer good only while quantities last. Offer available in Canada and the U.S. only. Request should be received no later than July 31, 2004. Each proof of purchase should be cut out of the back page ad featuring this offer.

Visit us at www.eHarlequin.com   FSPOP9R